THE WILL TO KILL

A MIKE HAMMER NOVEL

MORE MIKE HAMMER
FROM TITAN BOOKS

THE WILL TO KILL

A MIKE HAMMER NOVEL

MICKEY SPILLANE
and
MAX ALLAN COLLINS

TITANBOOKS

The Will to Kill: A Mike Hammer Novel
Mass-market edition ISBN: 9781783291434

Published by Titan Books
A division of Titan Publishing Group Ltd
144 Southwark St, London SE1 0UP

First mass-market edition: February 2018
1 3 5 7 9 10 8 6 4 2

A CIP catalogue record for this title is available from the British Library.

Printed and bound in the United States.

For Mickey's friend.

DAVID GUNDLING –

"He gives lawyers a good name!"

CO-AUTHOR'S NOTE

Once upon a time a thirteen-year-old Mickey Spillane fanatic grew up to be not just a friend of the great mystery writer, but a collaborator.

We worked together on comic books, anthologies, short stories, and a documentary. But novels were a form Mickey had no inclination to share with anybody—that was where he had made his fame and fortune, and that venue was his alone.

This changed in 2006 when, faced with rapidly failing health, he called to ask if I would finish his current Mike Hammer novel, *The Goliath Bone*—"if necessary." He also instructed his wife Jane to turn over his work files to me, including incomplete novels, several unproduced screenplays, and fragments that could be developed into short stories. Being so entrusted by the writer who had inspired me to become a writer myself was the greatest honor of my career.

The main task was finishing the Mike Hammer novels in progress. Hammer—"my bread and butter boy" as Mickey called him—had only appeared in thirteen novels published during Mickey's lifetime. Most fictional detectives of Mike Hammer's fame—Nero Wolfe, Perry Mason, Hercule Poirot—appeared in scores of novels. So expanding the Hammer canon using Mickey's own material became my first priority.

Six substantial manuscripts—of 100 pages or more, often with notes, sometimes with roughed-out endings—were my first order of business. These have all been completed. A number of shorter but significant Hammer manuscripts—again, sometimes with notes and rough endings—were also worthy of completion. *The Will to Kill* is the third of these.

This time I had only thirty pages or so from Mickey from which to develop the novel. But, as you will see, Mickey set everything nicely in motion in an unusual Mike Hammer mystery, the premise of which invokes none other than those of that other very tough-minded mystery writer, Agatha Christie.

Or maybe it's not so unusual. One of the characteristics of the Hammer novels, rarely commented upon, is that—sex and violence not withstanding—they are rather traditional mysteries at heart, tricky tales with clues fairly placed and unlikely villains who are hard to spot. Almost every Hammer novel includes a final chapter in which the detective faces down the murderer and explains every twist and turn of the plot.

One of the challenges of completing these novels is to figure out when Mickey began them, so I can keep them consistent with what he intended—Hammer and Spillane are ever-changing with the times and with age. A few of the manuscripts had dates on them, but most didn't. Some had pop-cultural references that helped fix the time frame or references to New York newspapers or restaurants having gone out of business.

This manuscript was tricky, with Mike and Pat clearly older (referring to each other as "old buddy") but World War II still a reference point (the first murder victim once worked in a defense plant). I have settled on around 1965 as my best guess.

M.A.C.

CHAPTER ONE

They came for the body at a quarter to four in the morning.

I had been looking at it for over an hour but hadn't bothered to call it in till not long ago. Some guys might have gone running into the night, looking for help or somewhere to puke. Me, I'd seen too much in my time to be shaken.

Anyway, there isn't much you can do for a man whose top half is lying on a jagged slab of ice that broke off from the main floe coming down the Hudson River to wedge itself against the pier.

And whose lower half isn't around.

Sometimes an oddity like that is a good point of focus when you have other things to think about and you can stare at such things for a long time while you clear away the roadblocks the world insinuates into your mind.

Like what was it about me that attracted death? What turned a reflective moment at the waterfront into a damn crime scene? And what put an ivory-washed half a corpse on a slab colder than the morgue tray awaiting it?

Behind me, the flashing red light of a squad car kept interrupting the brilliance of the full moon that had staged the little scene so well. One of the uniformed cops had already secured the chunk of ice while the other radioed in the situation before he walked back to me again.

He was blond and lanky, one of the new ones, still young enough to be dedicated, but experienced enough to be touched with that subtle cynicism that marks all the pros. When he flipped his book over to take down my story, his voice had that odd flat, casual tone ready to take note of everything, but disbelieve anything.

"Your name?"

"Mike Hammer."

"Full name Michael?"

"Right."

"Address?"

I gave it to him.

"You found the body?" he asked me.

I nodded.

"When?"

"Two-forty. I checked my watch."

He checked his. "It's now… ten after four."

"How about that."

His eyes flicked at me curiously. People don't find a

body and act that blasé about it. People don't lean up against a crate thinking about something else when a torso spilling out its contents is only a few feet away. Not people in a new suit and a raincoat carelessly slung over their shoulder, even when it's cold as hell out.

"Mind telling me what you were doing here, Mr. Hammer?"

"I'm a night walker," I said.

He wrote it down. More to be polite than anything else.

"Occupation?"

I grinned at him. "Buddy, if you don't know by now…"

But I didn't have to tell him. The other cop came out of the shadows with his hands buried under his overcoat armpits to warm them, saw me plainly for the first time and said, "Hi, Mike. I thought they said it was gonna warm up tonight."

"It did for a while," I said.

He was one of the old ones—bucket head, jug ears, sharp eyes. The dedication was still there, but the years of experience had turned the cynicism into resigned acceptance. He looked at his partner and said, "Meet yourself a celebrated public figure, Frank. The tabloids' favorite private dick."

Frank squinted at his partner as if the older man were nuts.

The old harness bull nodded my way, a smile tickling his thin lips. "He doesn't make the headlines he used to, but he's got more kills on him than a Bengal tiger, and yet he still keeps his P.I. ticket. Don't ask me how. Better you call Captain Chambers and tell him his boy's laying off another stiff on us."

"Look, Hal…"

He shook a forefinger at his young cohort. "Just can it and do what I told you, Frank. Even without that stiff on ice, the water could get choppy."

Frank sighed and went off to do as he'd been told.

Hal said, "How's it going, Mike?"

"Smoke's still coming out the chimney."

"Must be. You didn't always look this prosperous. Brooks Brothers? Burberry? Who says crime don't pay." He gestured toward the half body on its slab. "What's *this* bit?"

"You got me, friend," I said. "I'm standing here, catching a smoke, and enjoying the moon on the Hudson, when that ice slab moves in and, being a trained detective, I notice it has half a body on it."

He wasn't sure he was buying it, but he also wasn't sure he cared. "Anybody you know?"

I shrugged. "It's getting so I know more dead ones than I do live ones. But I don't think so."

"Want to take a closer look?"

"Why not?"

Half a person isn't a pleasant thing to see. There's something obscene about a foreshortened human who is only a head and shoulders, arms and belly. We looked down from the pier at the expressionless face turned sideways against the ice, one arm folded under his chest, the other sprawled out awkwardly in front of his head. The way the water lapped around the edges of the grotesque raft made it sound like the river was bored.

"No blood on the ice," the cop stated.

"Water probably washed it off."

"Wonder why there's only half of him."

I squatted down on the pier and had a look at the corpse. To make it easier, the cop turned his flashlight on the mess so I could see it better. There was a peculiar configuration to the lower part of the torso.

When I stood up, I said, "Looks like it was pinched. That ice is twelve inches thick, easy, and if a couple of floes came together, they could have snipped him in half like a paper cutter."

He winced but nodded. "They're going to have a hell of a time determining time of death in this weather," he said. "Recognize him or not?"

"Not."

He let the light play over the body again. "Looks pretty well-dressed. Decent suit on him and his clothes, what's left of 'em, don't seem messed up very much. He's taken a bash on the side of the head but that could have come from anything. Blood's been washed off there too. Screwy. Suppose he was a leaper?"

I answered him with a question. "How old do you figure him?"

"About sixty-some. Why?"

I shrugged, looking at the body again. "Somebody

that age would have been wearing an overcoat. You'd hate to catch cold on your way to pull the Dutch act."

He'd been around enough to see the absurd truth of that. "So maybe it was an accident. There's still ice on the roads and bridges upstate, and if he got flipped out of a car and landed on that ice…" He saw me smirking at him and stopped. "What's so funny?"

"You."

"Me?"

"Sure. You're still making excuses for the world. You've seen so much dirt, you've started hiding it under the rug."

He frowned just a little. "Just because Mike Hammer found him doesn't make this guy a murder victim."

"No. There are various possibilities."

This time the cop's face twisted into a puzzled frown. "Such as?"

"You know how a magician saws somebody in half?"

"Sure."

I grinned at him. "Maybe this guy was working with a beginner."

"Oh, hell, Mike," he said, grinning back.

By the time the lab crew had finished, the sun had eased up over the apartment houses and draped the area in a baleful gray. The two reporters on the night beat had shrugged the thing off pending investigation when they found out I was only a disinterested spectator and left me alone with Pat Chambers.

Pat didn't arrive till they were carting the body away in the morgue wagon. He was a big, rangy guy in a trenchcoat, blond with gray-blue eyes and in his late thirties like me. The only reason he was giving this his personal attention was because I was involved—that, and guys who make captain in the Homicide Division seem to have a perverted sense of curiosity.

When he was satisfied with the investigating officer's report, he walked back to me, stuck a cigarette in his mouth and let me light it. "Why the hell don't you go to bed at night like everybody else?"

"Somebody's got to check the debris in this river," I told him.

He looked at me over the flickering match. "Not at this hour." He blew a cloud of smoke past me, his face expressionless. In the east the dawn was coming up, outlining the irregular skyline. "You got anything going, Mike?"

I shrugged and lit myself up. "Just petty stuff. Nothing rating a half a corpse. What did you get on the guy?"

Pat shrugged and took another drag on the butt. "Accident or suicide," he said. "There was no wallet in his coat, but he may have carried it in his pants. No attempt was made to rip out any labels in his clothes. If we can't make him from his prints or photo, we can check through the laundry marks. He's got plenty of those, including two dry cleaner tags still on his jacket."

"Any money?"

"Some change in a side suitcoat pocket. But, like the wallet, he could have carried it in his pants pocket."

"So put out an APB for the other half of him."

"Very funny." He took a last pull on the cigarette and flipped it into the river. "Any opinion, Mike?"

"Probably an accident. He could have stalled his car up where there's snow and started walking. He's old enough to've had a heart attack and tumbled into the river. The ice could've done the rest. Why make a federal case out of it?"

Pat shrugged and glanced at me. "Because nature has given you a freak propensity for tripping over things that aren't just accidents."

"Not this time, old buddy," I said.

"That blow to the head—you aren't thinking blunt instrument?"

"Why should I think anything? You're the cop."

"You got no ideas at all?"

"Sure. Let's go have some breakfast."

"You can eat after finding that?"

"Why, you aren't hungry?"

We grabbed some bacon and eggs in Riker's on Sixth Avenue.

At NYPD HQ on Centre Street, I lounged with my milk-and-sugared coffee in the visitor's chair while

Pat sat behind his desk checking through the missing persons sheets without finding anything tallying with the description of the half-body. Then he took my statement for the files.

Just as I finished signing the report, McGee—a dumpy veteran detective who was better than he looked—knocked once and came in. He was in his shirtsleeves. With a nod to me, he laid a paper on Pat's desk.

"We have a make on the body in the river, Captain," McGee said, his voice a chesty rumble that seemed to come out of a well. "Guy's prints were on file from a defense job during the war. Harry's checking Social Security in Washington to see if they have a current address on him. Last one was in a building they tore down ten years ago."

Pat scanned the report quickly and nodded, and McGee went out. Then the Homicide captain looked at me with narrowed eyes. "Jamison Elder. Age would be sixty-four this year. Born in London, took out naturalization papers eighteen years ago. Former occupation, domestic and chauffeur. Prior to the defense job, he worked for Condon Hale out on the Island."

"Condon Hale—the moneybags inventor?"

"That's him," Pat said, nodding. "Out on Long Island."

"He's a crazy old coot, I hear."

"We should all be so crazy," he said. The phone rang and he reached for it.

The Medical Examiner had finished the preliminary

autopsy and was ready to state (as I already speculated) that the body had been pinched in half by an ice floe. There was a contusion on the head that could have rendered him unconscious, a result of a fall or (as Pat already speculated) the usual blunt instrument, but wasn't the primary cause of death.

"Death came from either exposure or being cut in half about the same time," Pat said, reporting what the M.E. had told him. "Frozen condition of the body makes it difficult to pinpoint an exact time of death, but a little speculation could narrow it down."

"So speculate."

"It's improbable that the body would have gone unseen all the previous day because of the constant traffic on and along the river. And if you factor in the tidal flow, it couldn't have been much more than twenty miles from the farthest point upriver."

I gave him a doubtful look. "It could have hugged the banks where nobody spotted it."

"Possibly. Anyway, give the M.E. a little time and he'll lay a time period on it. These odd kinds of deaths always fascinate the guy. Besides, what are you so interested for?"

"They fascinate me too," I said.

"Stick to live females, pal, with both their top and bottom halves."

"Reminds me of the joke about the two mermaids—"

Before I could finish, McGee again knocked at the open door and bulled in. He pulled an unlit cigar from his mouth and handed Pat another sheet.

"An easy one, Captain. Jamison Elder was employed as a butler on the Dunbar estate outside Monticello."

Pat's face furrowed. "Not *Chester* Dunbar?"

Where had I heard that name?

The detective nodded. "That's the one. Elder left yesterday, right after dinner, for a week's vacation… to go see a relative in Delaware. This morning the State Police found his car jammed into a snowbank at the east end of a covered bridge over a stream feeding into the Hudson. The family's pretty shook up about it. Elder had been with them a long time."

"Were the keys in the car?"

"Nope. It was locked tight. The state cop I talked to said it looked like Elder skidded in and got stuck, couldn't back out. The nearest phone is a place near the entrance to Bear Mountain Bridge, and he could have been heading there to get a wrecker." He paused and stuck the cigar back in his mouth. "That road runs along the embankment. He could have been flipped over by a passing car."

Pat was frowning. "Hit-and-run?"

"Could be," McGee said, with a who-gives-a-damn shrug. "A fender could have lifted him from below the waist."

I said, "I don't think so."

They both looked at me.

"He would have been wearing an overcoat," I said.

The dick shook his head. "Not necessarily. I checked

that out. The temperature got up over forty last night, and walking like that? Could've warmed him up, and he carried it."

I said, "Then you should advise the state boys to look around the area to find any coat Elder might've worn."

McGee glanced at Pat, who nodded his agreement.

"Will do," the dick said. "You need anything else, Captain?"

Pat shook his head. "No. Good job."

When the detective left, Pat was staring past me into nothing. Something was really eating him. He just sat there muttering, "Damn," again and again.

I looked at him sideways. "Okay, 'damn.' What's that supposed to mean?"

His eyes rolled. "Brother, you really know how to make waves."

"I didn't make the waves, that half a corpse did."

"Don't you remember Chester Dunbar?" he asked, sitting forward. "The millionaire who took on the black market trade during the war, and had enough dough and influence to get half a dozen crooked politicians bounced out on their butts into jail cells?"

"I missed the papers when I was in the Pacific."

"Well, right after the war, Dunbar's money backed that independent investigation of that kid… Christie? The young officer they accused of excessive force after he shot that guy during a hold-up?"

"Yeah—I do remember that. Vaguely."

"Hell, they would have nailed Christie to the wall to please the bleeding hearts and the local politicians, if Dunbar hadn't forced the issue."

I shifted in my hard chair. "So he was a good citizen. Sounds like he could afford to be. What are you all worked up about?"

Pat's eyes were distant, his expression somber. "Because Dunbar used to be a cop, Mike. A damn good one. Back when you and I first got out of the academy, he was my precinct captain. That initial year, he guided me through some rough patches, really put me on the right path."

I was nodding. "Right. I remember now. I met Dunbar a few times. But didn't he quit the force in the late '40s?"

Pat nodded. "Dunbar was one of these home-grown inventors, ever since he was a kid—always experimenting and fooling around in his basement workshop. That Condon Hale character was a kind of mentor. Well, believe it or not, he invented an electronic gizmo that modulated radio frequencies to control torpedoes. During the war, he let the government have the rights for the duration. But after that, he cleaned up on it. Invented lots of other profitable stuff, too. Like the pacemaker, which would come in handy for you if you had a heart."

So that was how an ex-cop became a millionaire.

"For a while," Pat said, "he worked with that Hale character, but it didn't last long. Bad blood over an invention both men claimed as theirs. But that must be how Chet met Jamison Elder… when Elder was Hale's butler."

I said, "I'm sure your pal Chet'll be sorry to see his butler go. But otherwise, how's a probable accidental death going to bother him?"

Pat leaned across the desk, his face serious, his eyes intense. "It won't bother him one small bit, old buddy. Chester Dunbar's been dead three years. Had a heart attack one night and couldn't get to his nitro capsules in time. He was on the floor, where he'd been crawling toward the bathroom and the pills. The coroner up there ruled *that* accidental death too."

"So?"

Pat's mouth was a thin, hard line. "Chet never took a chance like that in his life! He used to keep two spare pills on him at all times, in case the bottle was out of reach."

"Even in his pajamas?"

"Even there. They weren't on him that night."

I sat forward. "Wasn't that enough to prompt an investigation?"

His mouth twisted in a scornful grimace. "Yes, but there was enough to stop it before it began. Chet complained of chest pains that afternoon, and had his medicine brought to him, and retired to his room to rest and get feeling better. The next time he was seen… he was dead. There were still traces of nitro in his body, so it was assumed that he'd had another attack, used the spares and lay down, then had another, more serious, attack later. Apparently couldn't make it to the bottle on a table by where he'd been reading earlier. And that was all she wrote."

"Sounds possible."

"Not when you knew Chet." He rocked back in his swivel chair, staring past me at the wall. "The books are closed on it, Mike… but the smell's still there."

"It's out of your jurisdiction, Pat."

"You're telling me."

"I get it. I do get it. You see a second accidental death and the accidental part starts to bug you."

"It does."

"So what else is bugging you about it?"

"I don't know, Mike. Chet's kids, maybe."

"Somebody got anxious to inherit, you think? Sounds like he had plenty of loot."

"Oh, he did, but my understanding is that everybody's taken care of. Equal shares."

"Equal suspects. You know these kids?"

"Somewhat."

"So what's the rundown, Pat?"

He grunted something like a laugh. "Two are bums, one's beautiful, and one's a congenital idiot."

I almost laughed myself. "That's a hell of a summary. How about a little more?"

With a look of disgust, he elaborated: "Dexter and Wake were his late wife's kids by a previous marriage. Their own father was already dead, and Chet adopted them legally after he and their mother got married.

Those two are in their mid-thirties and have lived off their father's wealth forever. Lovely Dorena was the Dunbar couple's first natural child. Three years later they had Charles, 'Chickie,' they call him. His wife died having the boy. Chet was never the same."

"Tough."

"Damn right," Pat said. He sighed. "The law firm of Hines & Carroll has been taking care of the estate since Chet died. The mansion is, well, it's a damn *mansion*, and they all live there, the kids—adult children, I should say, and you can take that any way you like. Until now, though, everything's been going along pretty well." He sighed heavily. "I would hate like hell to see the papers make anything of Elder's death."

"What difference does it make?"

Pat shrugged. "I just know Chet wouldn't have wanted the publicity. He turned reclusive after the retarded boy was born. They've been protecting Chickie since they found out he was… special. Kind of keeping the lid on. You see, the other Dunbars are still in the social swing, and I doubt if more than half a dozen people know about there being the likes of Chickie in the family."

"Not an easy secret to keep."

"Maybe so, but they pretty much kept it. You know what really used to bother Chet? Ever since she was very small, Dorena has been scared to death of marriage… for fear of adding another subnormal member to the family. That could be a rough damn prospect to live with—not just for Dorena, but Chet, who would dearly have loved to have grandchildren."

"Hell, Pat, didn't Dunbar check this slow kid out with the medical people?"

"Oh, he had Chickie thoroughly checked out, as much as possible. But it's still uncertain whether it's a congenital condition or one of those things that happened with a difficult labor. One doctor even suggested possible brain damage from improper use of forceps during the delivery, but refused to be quoted on it."

I said, "The possibility of malpractice probably had the medics covering each other's tails."

Pat didn't contradict that. "Funny thing is, Chet's hope was that it *was* accidental." He fired up another cigarette and took a deep pull on it. "And now here we are… with *another* goddamn accident."

I was shaking my head. "Pat, these things don't have anything to do with each other—a possible accident at birth in delivery, a heart patient who didn't take his medicine, a family retainer who likely had an automobile accident?"

But I was remembering what I'd said to that cop at the scene: *You're still making excuses for the world. You've seen so much dirt, you've started hiding it under the rug.*

"If nothing else," Pat said, "I ought to express my condolences as a friend of the family… You doing anything today?"

"Lunch date with Velda," I said.

Velda was my secretary, a P.I. herself, and my partner in several ways.

"Cancel it," he said, "and let's take a run up there."

"I thought you *wanted* me to stick with live females."

"Both halves of her will still be intact," he said, "when we get back."

CHAPTER TWO

You came over the crest of the hill and saw the Dunbar estate snowbound in all its formal elegance like something on a Christmas card. Winter ivy relieved the stark gray stones of the outer wall and buildings, the pines towering past the roof peaks, the only motion the thin wisps of wood smoke that rose wraith-like from two of the massive chimneys.

Overhead the sun made the snow sparkle with a weird brilliance, burning it from the roadbeds to run bubbling into drainage ditches. A mile away a horseshoe bend in the Hudson River was a jigsaw puzzle of broken ice flowing toward the Atlantic from the spring thaw that had hit farther upstate.

We drove up to the wrought-iron gates and waited while a slight figure in his fifties in a black-and-white-and-red plaid hunter's jacket and a matching cap with ear flaps came crunching in galoshes through the snow out of the fieldstone guardhouse on the left and inspected us both through the bars.

Leaning on the wheel, Pat said, "That's Willie Walters. He used to be a jailer in the Tombs. Got retired out early and was having a hard time of it till Chet put him back on his feet with a caretaker job here."

I took in the looming gates. "He must like being behind bars."

Pat grinned at me. "Hell, man, that's the ultimate in socialism. They tell you where and when to go, what to do and how to do it. You're clothed, fed, numbered, and protected behind a wall. What a feeling of security. It's a wonder you haven't tried it yet."

"Drop dead," I said pleasantly.

Pat got out and spoke to the slender caretaker, getting a watery look of recognition in sky-blue eyes and an enthusiastic handclasp through the gate. Willie Walters had a face wrinkled beyond his years and a pointed chin that gave him a Punch-and-Judy look. He waved Pat and me through the gates, leaving them ajar with the car still outside. Just inside, my friend introduced me to Walters before asking him, "Anything new on Elder?"

"Naw. Got the body in New York yet, ain't they?"

What was left of it.

"In the morgue," Pat said.

The caretaker's voice was high-pitched and raspy, like a table saw. "Heard them two boys arguing about which one has to go down there to identify him. Guess

Wake's goin' in to do that later."

I said, "'Boys?' Aren't the Dunbar brothers both in their thirties?"

"That they are," Walters said. "But they're still a couple of kids, you ask me. About a year apart, Dex the older. Them two are pissers! Wake fancies himself as some kinda artist, and Dex goes into town now and then to a little office, tendin' his investments. Really, neither one wants to do nothin' but drink and spend money and chase tail—even Wake, the married one!"

"Everybody needs a hobby," I said.

"What gets me is that Jamie's been here almost twenty years, like a part of the family, and them punks don't even give a rat's ass that he's dead!"

Pat asked, "How about Dorena?"

"Oh, she's the best of a bad lot. You can tell she really cares—her and Jamison was friendly, in a servant and master kinda way." He shook his head and the ear flaps flapped. "But it's Chickie what's really shook up about it. Jamie like to raise him from a pup. Mr. Dunbar just let Jamie take charge of the boy… even fixed up the old carriage house so they could live there together. I'm up there, too."

"You said 'boy' again," I said. "How old is Chickie, anyway?"

"Twenty. But he's half that in his mind." Walters sighed, staring at his toes. "Don't know *what* that kid's gonna do now. Dorena, she's good with him, really loves the boy, but she's got her own life to live… the others? They don't even make out like he's alive."

Pat nodded toward the mansion-like structure. "Everybody up at the house?"

"Sure are—*at* each other, like usual. Them lawyers are comin' out later. Mr. Dunbar had us all in the will, you know—me and Jamie, I mean. We were the only full-time live-in staff, but there's a cook, a maid, and some cleaning gals from town. All colored."

I asked, "What are the 'kids' at each other about?"

He sighed again but there was a weary laugh in it. "Hell's bells, they fight about *everything*! I think they're mostly scared somebody's gonna poke their noses in here 'cause of Jamie buying it. You'd think he done it on purpose! But what *I* think is they're afraid somebody's gonna open up Mr. Dunbar's death for another look-see."

Pat asked, "Why, Willie—do you suspect foul play where Chester Dunbar is concerned?"

He held up mittened hands of surrender. "I said too much already. I'm just a hired hand—what the hell do I know? But what a bunch those kids is! Good thing Chet left a will they couldn't break, or they'd have tangled asses all over the place, scratchin' after his dough."

Pat threw me a glance, then said to the caretaker, "What about Jamie Elder, Willie? You think *that* was an accident?"

The caretaker snorted. "Well, he sure didn't take *himself* out! Jamie liked it here; pay was good, room and board was free, and Chickie was like his own kid. He woulda never took a week of vacation if his sister wasn't sick. He kinda got it in his head that she was on her last legs, and there was no stopping him."

Pat nodded. "Who was supposed to take care of Chickie while Jamie was gone?"

"Ah, the kid ain't no trouble nohow. Sits and watches TV, plays with kid toys. Gardens all the time, when he can. That's all he knows and understands, really. Maybe he wasn't born with much of a brain, but he's sure got a green thumb—digs plants, trims bushes. I taught him that. When the thaw comes, he'll be back at it."

"Still," Pat said, "it sounds like young Chickie'll be lost without Jamie."

"Won't be easy on him. But Dorena looks out for him pretty good, and sometimes the boy comes down here and we mess around some, tossin' a ball around. Like I say, I stay up in the carriage house with him—so did Jamie. But right now, they moved me down here…" He nodded to the modest fieldstone guardhouse. "…to stay on the gates round-the-clock, in case anybody comes pokin' around, sticking their nose in. You know, reporters and sightseers and such."

I offered the old man a cigarette, took one myself, and said, "You said it hit Chickie hard about Elder, Willie. Who broke the news to him?"

The wizened face scowled as he lighted up the Lucky. "It was Dexter—*that* bum! It was almost like he *enjoyed* it. Chickie's twenty years old but he bawled like a baby. Did the same thing when the dog was killed, and when them lousy kids drowned those ducks in the pond."

"Someday he'll kick back at Dexter," I said.

Pat gave me a wry grin and shook his head. "Not likely, Mike. Unfortunately, Chickie's deficient physically as well as mentally. He can't weigh over a hundred-twenty pounds and only comes up to my shoulder."

"Smaller than that have got even," I pointed out.

Pat shrugged, flipped his cigarette into the driveway, then stared up at the big house. "Okay, Willie, keep doing what you're doing and don't let in any strangers. But if Corporal Sheridan from the State Police stops by, well, of course send him up."

"Will do, Captain." He squinted at Pat and me and managed a feeble smile. "Glad you come by. Feels like old times. You, uh… don't think somebody murdered ol' Jamie, do you?"

"Don't know," Pat said. "What's your opinion, Willie?"

The wrinkled puss scrunched in thought. "Well, I can't think of a soul who'd want to do harm to that kind ol' feller. But on the other hand, that bunch up at the house? Who knows *what* they might do."

We drove up the long, gently winding drive that led to a four-car garage that was of much more recent vintage than the house itself, though fashioned of similar stone. A walk curved around to the front door where we pounded the snow from our shoes on the welcome mat and Pat pressed the doorbell, which set some chimes going.

A wisp-of-a-thing Negro maid in standard black-trimmed white livery greeted us. We were expected— Pat had called ahead. She took our hats and coats and gestured toward the living room that yawned past a ballroom-ceilinged entry area bigger than my apartment, a stairway curving up and out of sight.

The walls in this place were off-white, the woodwork white with a column effect at the doorless doorways. The floor was a burnished parquet, and only the furnishings, rather bland if expensive '40s contemporary, suggested this near-mansion had been the home of an ex-cop. Everywhere downstairs was high-ceilinged and the living room, where Pat and I entered, had a flower-petal chandelier and a built-in, good-size fireplace, which was licking and snapping.

Near the fire on facing couches a man and a woman lounged on each. One pair were clearly brother and sister, their narrow faces with aquiline nose, big brown eyes, and full sensual mouth mirroring each other. Both were blond, and only their attire and the young woman's lightly applied make-up and chin-length hair set them apart.

She wore a camel tan sheath dress with a darker leather belt and a jaunty brown beret. He wore an oversize rust-suede sweater with beige woolen arms and turtleneck, and new blue jeans that I doubted would ever look worn.

The two across from them were almost certainly not related, although the male bore some resemblance to the pair seated across from him, his face more oval than narrow and his hair dark. He wore the kind of outfit that can get a guy punched in the mouth—a navy-blue linen blazer with a matching ascot and pink shirt. The female was tall and voluptuous, a pale-blue-eyed redhead in a green mini-dress and darker green nylons—the kind of outfit that can get a girl punched in the mouth… with a guy's lips.

Nobody seemed to be much in mourning for the late Jamison Elder, despite Willie Walters saying the departed had been "like part of the family."

The ascot-wearer said, "Captain Chambers—please join us. Sit, sit."

That seemed a good idea, since neither hosts nor hostesses had stood. A couple of comfortable chairs were awaiting us, facing the fire across a low-slung coffee table, and we took them. They were having drinks—cocktails, wine. Apparently we weren't.

"Thanks for seeing me," Pat said. "I know Mr. Elder's death must be a real blow to you."

The blond guy in the oversize sweater said to Pat, "Who's your friend?"

There was something nasty about it.

I said, "Mike Hammer."

The blonde in the beret sat forward, big brown eyes wide, and said, "You're the one who found the body."

What there was of it.

THE WILL TO KILL

I nodded. "Captain Chambers and I are old friends. I'm just keeping him company."

Pat said, "Sorry, Mike—I better make the introductions."

He did. The oversize-sweater guy was Wakefield "Wake" Dunbar, and seated across from him was his brother Dexter "Dex" Dunbar. The beret-wearing beauty was their half-sister Dorena, and the tall curvy redheaded thing in half a skirt was Madeline, Wake's wife.

Interesting—Wake was sitting with his sister, while Dex was sitting with Wake's wife. Probably didn't mean anything, but detectives take in details like that.

Pat said, "Wake, I understand you're coming into the city to identify the body. I can arrange that with the morgue for you."

Wake, whose expression was wary, said, "Thank you, Captain Chambers. Tomorrow morning all right? We have lawyers coming this evening."

"Sure."

Flickering reflection on his face emphasized his slight sneer. "But you didn't have to drive almost two hours to tell me that. What's the purpose of this visit? And I think we all know who Mike Hammer is."

Pat began to reply, but Dex beat him to it. "Wake, for God's sake, Captain Chambers is a family friend. He knows how close we all were to Jamison, and he's here to express his condolences." Dex turned to Pat. "Isn't that right, Captain Chambers?"

"That *is* right," Pat said. "But I thought, since Mr.

Hammer here discovered Mr. Elder's remains—and being as I was called to the scene—that you might have some questions."

Dorena said, "Did he suffer? Please tell me he didn't suffer." Her eyes were wet. She meant it.

Wake said, with the smirk getting nastier, "Somebody cut him in half, sis. That *has* to smart."

"Damnit, Wake," Dex began. "There's no call—"

I interrupted, "Nobody cut anybody in half. Elder suffered a blow to the head, wound up on an ice floe, and expired due to exposure and loss of blood. That's straight from the Medical Examiner. Another ice floe caused the damage to the body."

Wake grunted something like a laugh and said, "You mean half of him is still out there somewhere, don't you?"

"The rest of him will turn up," I said cheerfully. "When the bloat kicks in."

A gentle hand came to Dorena's horrified open mouth. Her pink nail polish matched her lipstick, I noted.

Pat gave me a sideways look, then said to the little group, "I just wanted you people to know that if you have any questions or concerns—either individually or as a group—you can come to me. As I think you know, I thought the world of your late father."

The stunning redhead wore a faint look of amusement. Her lashes were long, her eyeshadow white. "Elder was just a hired hand, Mr., uh, Chambers is it? We don't need any grief counseling. But thanks."

Dex frowned at her, but her husband was smiling over at her. They both thought this was funny somehow. Even if they didn't sit together.

Dorena said, "We just thought... when you called and wanted to come up and see us... that you might be acting in your... official capacity."

"Yes," Wake said, still with a hint of sneer. "You *are* a captain of Homicide, aren't you? We were told this was an accidental death, and now you come around with the redoubtable Michael Hammer at your side. Did somebody get murdered?"

With a sigh, Dex sat forward, hands clasped between his open knees, and said, "Captain Chambers, I hope you'll forgive my brother for his flippant attitude. But he's right that we all viewed your request to come and see us as a kind of... red flag. Could Jamison's death have been a homicide?"

"It hasn't been ruled out," Pat admitted, "but it may be. There'll be an inquest—"

"Christ," Wake interrupted, "will one of us have to attend *that*, as well? Isn't it enough of an inconvenience that this body identification has been deemed necessary?"

Pat, staying remarkably cool, said, "None of you will be required to attend the inquest. When it's scheduled, I'll let you know... but attending would be entirely voluntary."

Dex said, "Thank you, Captain. But you haven't

answered my question—in your expert opinion, *could* this have been a homicide?"

Pat glanced at me and I shrugged.

Then he said, "Jamison suffered a blow on the head that might have been from a blunt instrument. But it also just as easily could have been the result of a minor automobile accident."

Dorena, sitting forward, said, "We were told they found his car stuck in a snowbank."

Wake said to her, "Not his car, *our* car." Then to Pat, he clarified, "One of ours. Jamison had use of it, and we allowed him to take it on this trip home to see his sick sister. Is she coming to pick up her brother, by the way? If so, maybe *she* could identify the body."

This guy was a real winner.

Pat said, "We haven't got a hold of her yet. But as Mr. Hammer said, Jamison Elder died of exposure and loss of blood."

"But," Dorena said, "if somebody hit him with a... a pipe or something, and it led to his death... that would be *murder*... wouldn't it?"

Dumb question, but she was upset.

Pat nodded, then added, "But my guess is, it'll be ruled accidental."

"Your guess," Wake said, unimpressed.

"Educated guess. If there's any change of status... if the coroner's inquest does not declare this death accidental... I'll let you know immediately."

Wake asked, "How badly damaged was the car?"

Pat shrugged. "Not very, if at all. It just got stuck in the snow."

"How do we go about getting it back?"

What a guy.

Dex said, "For Christ's sake, Wake! Have a little common decency."

Wake smirked at his brother.

Pat said, patiently, "I'll look into that and let you know."

Arms folded, I said, "Where's the other brother? Charles? Chickie?"

Wake rolled his eyes in a who-gives-a-damn fashion.

Dorena said, "Chickie's in his room. Out in the carriage house."

I said, "Shouldn't somebody be looking after him?"

Her chin came up a little. "He's not helpless, Mr. Hammer. But he's very upset… shattered, really… about Jamison's passing." She looked at Pat. "Captain Chambers, perhaps you could say a word to him. I know, back when Father was alive and you would visit, you and Chickie got along famously."

"I'd like to say hello to the boy, yes," Pat said.

I was looking forward to that myself. Their outcast brother had been described as an idiot. But plenty of those were walking the streets. And at least one was sitting on a sofa nearby.

Dorena stood and so did Pat and I. We nodded farewells to the rest of this lovely group and followed the shapely little blonde—and she *was* little, maybe five-foot-four—through a book-lined library to French doors onto the outside.

She turned to us with a smile. It was a nice smile. For this family, it was a great one.

"I don't think you'll need your coats," she said. "It's not much of a walk."

"It's warming up, anyway," I said.

We followed her in crisp afternoon air over a fieldstone path back to a two-story gray-stone carriage house that at one time had been converted to a two-car garage, then converted again to living quarters. Beyond the carriage house and hugging its back wall was Chickie's garden that Walters had mentioned, largely snow-covered right now.

As we went inside, she said, "The downstairs was mostly Jamison's—his bedroom's in back."

We were in a kind of recreation room with comfy chairs, a braid rug, and a good-size TV; a gas fireplace was in a corner, and a kitchenette area off to one side. Some built-in bookcases ran to popular paperbacks— *Forever Amber*, *The Carpetbaggers*, *Lolita*, plus a good stack of *Playboy*s. For an old bachelor, Jamison had pretty racy taste. Maybe at his age that was the only way to get his jollies.

She led us up a circular wrought-iron staircase to a little landing off of which were two doors; the view of her nice bottom working like pistons under the snug sheath dress wasn't bad at all.

As she knocked on the door directly at the top,

she nodded toward the other one. "That's where the caretaker sleeps. Walters." She knocked again, harder. "...Chickie! Chickie, it's your big sister. Open up. There are some friends here to see you."

Finally the door opened and a boy about the same size as the girl stood there expressionlessly. Not a boy at all, really, as the blue shadow of a morning shave said he was well into puberty. That jarred with what he wore—pajamas whose white knit top bore a red-and-black ski-sweater pattern, the red bottoms tapered above blue-and-red slippers with another winter design.

"Can we come in, honey?" she asked.

He nodded. His face vaguely recalled his sister's, his eyes big and blank and bloodshot, his hair a dark fringe. He turned his back to us and disappeared into the room.

His quarters must have taken up two-thirds of the space of the second floor. The ceiling had a slant, reflecting the roof, and from it hung various model airplanes at rakish angles. In one corner was a tee-pee; on a white built-in counter sat a globe and a scattering of comic books—*Batman*, *Spiderman*, *Hulk*—near bookends gripping two feet of Hardy Boys novels under a shelf that held footballs and a baseball glove with ball. A shelf above that displayed more model airplanes and a collapsible telescope, a regular Long John Silver spy glass.

The overall trappings were western—a wooden bed with wagon wheels and a Lone Ranger bed spread, a nightstand with a rearing horse lamp. But the plane motif was providing competition with the Wild West, framed pictures of vintage aircraft staggered over the headboard.

I looked around and the boy was gone.

No—he was in the tee-pee, appropriately enough sitting Indian-style.

Dorena walked over and we followed. Bending down, hands on her knees, she said, "Chickie, honey, sweetie— you remember Captain Chambers, don't you?"

She gestured to Pat ringmaster fashion and he stepped forward.

The boy scrambled out of the tee-pee and hugged Pat. Hard.

"Whoa, there, cowboy," Pat said. Chickie did not release his grip. Pat tousled the boy's hair. "You've had a pretty bad shock, haven't you, kiddo?"

The boy let loose of him and went quickly to his bed and sat on the edge, facing away from us. He was nodding. Pat sat next to him.

"It's not easy when you lose somebody," Pat said. "You really liked Mr. Elder, didn't you?"

"…Jamie was nice." The voice was deep. A man's voice. But the cadence was childish.

"That's what you called him? Jamie?"

The boy nodded.

"He lived here with you."

Another nod.

"I guess he was your teacher. And your friend."

Another.

"Like I said, it's tough losing somebody."

"I lost Daddy."

"I know. He was my good friend. And I hope we're still friends, Chickie, you and I."

"Been a long time."

Pat's sigh was heavy with regret. "Right. I haven't been a very good friend, not lately. Maybe I can do better."

"Move in here, maybe?"

Pat put a hand on the boy's shoulder. "No, I can't. I have a job in the city."

The boy's face swung to Pat. "You're a policeman!"

"You remembered."

"Do you have your gun?"

"Not with me."

"Can I shoot it some time?"

"We'll see. Let me introduce you to somebody. This is my friend Mike Hammer. He's a real-life private eye."

He craned to look at me with childish awe. "Like on TV!"

"Not exactly," I said, smiling.

"Do *you* have a gun?"

"Yes, Chickie."

"Do you have it with you?"

I nodded. "Want to see it?"

He was smiling now, a ten-year-old's smile in the twenty-year-old face. "I want to hold it!"

I got the .45 out from the shoulder sling. I removed the clip—often I kept one in the chamber, but things had been slow lately, and anyway Velda had been on me about the danger of that practice.

From the other side of the bed, I passed him the weapon. He held it tentatively in a hand that didn't close around it. Dorena was standing near the foot of the bed, fig-leafed, frowning a little. Big sisters don't like it when father figures encourage boys to play with guns. Particularly real guns.

"Can I shoot this some time, Mr., uh… what's your name?"

"Call me Mike."

"Okay, Mike. Can I shoot it sometime?"

"Maybe. We'll have to ask your sister."

She was looking at him and slowly shaking her head.

I grinned at him. "You'll have to work on her. Listen, son—are you all right? Like Captain Chambers says—it's a hard one, losing a friend like you did."

"Is Jamie in heaven, Mike?"

"Was he a nice man?"

"Real nice."

"Then you bet he's in heaven."

This time he scrambled across the Lone Ranger and hugged me. Dorena was wiping a tear away. I hugged the big little boy back.

"You send a prayer up," I said, "for your friend Jamie, okay, son? Tonight?"

He nodded a bunch of times.

As we were on our way out, he took my hand. "Mike,

did you ever kill an Indian?"

I chuckled. "No, the Indians are our friends now. Like the Lone Ranger's pal Tonto. You have a tee-pee, don't you? So you know that they're a great and good people."

But the boy was clearly disappointed.

I said, "I did tangle with a Russian once who looked like an Indian. But I didn't shoot him."

I just nailed his hand to a barn floor so a federal friend of mine could have him.

Dorena told Chickie she'd be back in a while to collect him for supper. He gave both Pat and me another hug and scurried back to his tee-pee.

Outside, dusk had fallen, and it was colder.

Dorena said, "Would you and Mr. Hammer like to stay for supper? We have an excellent cook."

"Very generous of you," Pat said, "but we have that two-hour drive ahead of us. We'll catch a bite on the way. Listen, is there any hope for that young man?"

She breathed deep, in and out. "My father always prayed there would be. There are no outward signs of retardation, and medical breakthroughs are happening every day. Jamison home-schooled him right here, and Chickie's up to a fifth-grade level now."

I asked, "Who will teach him now?"

"I think possibly I will. Not that I'm qualified, but…"

"But you love him," I said.

She nodded, swallowed, eyes teary again.

In the car, Pat said, "She's the best of the bunch, isn't she?"

"No question. But I think we both know that's faint praise."

We didn't talk much on the way home. I could tell Pat was troubled and going over in his mind everything we'd heard and seen.

Me, I just kept hearing that asshole Wake asking…

…*Did somebody get murdered?*

CHAPTER THREE

The snow was rain now, making the city a messy morning thing that wasn't winter any more but sure as hell wasn't spring. Wetness trailed down the office windows in ghostly fingers, shimmering and shifting and writing messages no one could read.

Velda was already at her desk when I shut the door behind me and hung the drenched Dobbs porkpie hat and the soaked Burberry raincoat in the closet. Back at the old Hackard Building, our coat tree would've had to do, spilling a puddle onto where the floor had long since been ruined. But these were our new, nicer (though probably temporary) digs, while the old girl called Hackard got a facelift.

The set-up here was much the same, although the outer office was bigger and more inviting, with lots of dark wood paneling and a leather couch and matching chairs. The reception area walls were arrayed with framed newspaper and magazine stories about Velda's boss, as well as some sharpshooting plaques and civic awards. Her desk was centered, her back to the door to my inner office. All we'd brought with us from the Hackard were two metal file cabinets and the little scarred wooden table with the coffee maker and room for goodies, like the Danish she had waiting for me.

I hadn't said hello and neither had she, studying an inside page of the *Daily News*. She was frowning, but that took nothing away from her dark-eyed beauty framed by a shoulder-brushing, raven-wing black, fashion-be-damned pageboy.

Even seated, her stature was obvious; but she had fuller, higher breasts than most tall girls, and with her narrow waist and those endless long legs, she could make a white blouse and black skirt look worthy of Lily St. Cyr.

And yet somehow I got work done in this place.

Thinking about how professional of me that was, I helped myself to a cardboard cup of coffee, gave it sugar and milk, and wrapped my Danish in a paper napkin and nibbled and sipped as I strolled over to the client chair facing her.

"I hope," I said, sitting, "you greet prospective customers more warmly."

"Have you seen this?" she asked, lowering the tabloid enough to peer over it at me. That voice of hers was as liquid as the coffee, and right now just as hot.

"Just the funnies," I said.

"You made Page Three."

"I only pay attention when I make Page One."

She put the paper down. She was irritated, a condition she could convey without wrinkling her face. Remarkable. "You found a *body* yesterday, and you didn't even call me about it?"

I shrugged. Sipped. "It was just half a body."

"Oh. Well, that's different. That's something else entirely." She gestured to the *News*. "Did you tell this reporter that you planned to find the killer and go off on one of your murder hunts?"

"Let me see that," I said, and put the coffee and Danish down, then grabbed the paper.

A grim picture of the half a body covered with a blanket, on a stretcher, getting hauled up into the ambulance by orderlies, was accompanied by a smaller shot of Pat and me talking at the scene.

"Notice I'm not quoted," I said. "I didn't talk to any of the newshounds. Seemed like when they found out I just happened onto this partial stiff, they lost interest."

"Well, this guy," she said, "thought about it a while, then figured different."

I was glancing at the piece. "He's dredged up all the old cases. This is just a rehash of every self-defense plea I pulled in the last twenty years."

She was looking at me carefully. "So *are* you taking this on?"

"Taking what on? It's probably going to be ruled accidental."

"Give me a break. Somebody sapped the guy and pushed him in the river! Just because you were off on one of your insomniac night prowls and stumbled onto this poor half a bird, that doesn't mean you have to find the killer. You didn't know this, this… Jamison Elder, right? So why get involved?"

"Exactly," I said, tossing the *News* back on her desk and retrieving my coffee and Danish.

She was giving me a look as wide-eyed as some hick in a swamp spotting a flying saucer. Finally she managed, "Say what?"

"I didn't know the guy, Vel. It's none of my business, none of my concern. Let the cops earn some of my tax dollars for a change."

A tapering red-nailed finger tapped the tabloid. "Looks like you and Pat were talking up a storm at the scene. You don't come off very unconcerned in that photo."

"Well, Pat has a connection to this. I was just being a sounding board."

"Explain."

I leaned forward. "Remember I told you I had to skip lunch with you at the Blue Ribbon yesterday? That Pat wanted me to accompany him on business upstate?"

"Yes, of course. But that's *all* you told me."

I told her the rest, filled her in on our visit to the Dunbar estate, including the charming family members we'd encountered. Well, Dorena hadn't been so bad. Or Chickie.

"So you have no stake in this," she said.

"None. Like I said, Pat does, and it's his case. That partial corpse beached itself here in Manhattan, didn't it?"

She looked thoughtful. "Might not be his jurisdiction, if they determine this Elder character died upstate and just floated into your lap later."

I shrugged. "Pat has friends in the state cops. If that's the case, he'll lean on them to do right. You don't seem anxious for me to get involved."

"No kidding. This thing literally drifts into your lap, right when we've been getting back on our feet financially, and it's actually looking like Michael Hammer Investigations might be a going concern again. After our... absence."

She was referring to a small matter of seven years spent by her behind the Iron Curtain, spying for Uncle Whiskers, during which time I'd crawled into a bottle, thinking she was dead and I'd caused it. Every couple has the occasional misunderstanding.

The lovely features softened. "I don't mean to get in your personal business, Mike. I know if somebody needs help, or... well, you feel you need to get even... that you're going to wade right in. But we don't need to borrow trouble with something like this. Where your presence is strictly coincidental."

"I couldn't agree more."

She was studying me the way a scientist does a slide under a microscope lens. "You *mean* that."

"I do. I have absolutely no reason, no motivation, to get involved in this. I mean, come on, doll—you know I need a whole corpse to get interested. A half a one just doesn't cut it."

That made her smile. Even made her chuckle a little.

"Okay," she said. "All that insurance paperwork is waiting on your desk, and there are six phone calls for you to return from clients, current and potential. Have a blast."

I chewed the last bite of the Danish, swallowed it, got up and said, "It's nice being a going concern. Just no damn fun."

She didn't disagree with me.

Velda and I were seated at our favorite table in the bar at the Blue Ribbon Restaurant on West Forty-fourth Street, tucked in a corner overseen by two walls of autographed celebrity pictures. I was working on the knockwurst platter and Velda on a shrimp salad when somebody came over who wasn't a waiter.

"I hoped I might find you here," Pat Chambers said.

He had his rain-dripping hat off but his trenchcoat, still on, looked like it was crying.

"Sit down, buddy," I said. "Pull up a chair. Take off your coat and stay a while."

He did and the bartender, George, materialized with a pilsner of Pabst for him. Did Captain Chambers want anything to eat? He did not.

In fact, he looked too preoccupied to eat or maybe even breathe. His eyes were red and his complexion was gray. He did not bother to acknowledge Velda, which said something, since he was half-crazy about her.

"Pat," I said, pushing my plate aside. "What is it?"

"I don't have jurisdiction in the Elder case."

I glanced at Velda, whose eyes widened momentarily as if to say, *I told you so.*

"The NYPD and the state cops," he said, "have agreed that the matter should be kept upstate. Even the inquest will be there."

"But you didn't agree."

"I wasn't asked. The determination was that the cause of death is linked to the apparent accident on the Sullivan County end. The only saving grace here is that Corporal Jim Sheridan will be in charge of the investigation."

"Friend of yours?"

Pat nodded. "A good man. But all this talk of an 'accident' doesn't encourage me. Mike, I know from time to time I've encouraged you to stay out of ongoing police investigations—"

"Yeah, once or twice."

Velda had her eyes closed. She knew what was coming.

"But this time," Pat said, leaning forward, "I need your help. I can't get involved without really getting my tail in a sling. Could you do the job I can't?"

"Not without a client, I can't."

"You'll have a client."

"Who?"

"Me."

Velda opened her eyes.

I said, "What exactly do you want me to do, old buddy?"

"I want you to look into both of these 'accidental' deaths—Chet Dunbar, three years ago, and Jamison Elder, just the other day. It's possible they are accidental, and if that's the conclusion you reach, I'll live with it. If Mike Hammer can't sniff out murder, nobody can."

"Pat, I don't want your money. I'll do this as a favor, but—"

"I'm your client. Treat me no differently. I'll pay your $150 a day."

"No you won't. I'll have Velda draw up a contract, as usual through our lawyer. It'll be legal as hell. I'll require a one-dollar retainer."

His frown was a mixture of embarrassment and frustration. "Mike... Mike, that's not what I'm after."

"What you're after is the truth of this thing, right?"

"...Right." He sighed, shook his head. "I won't be there, man. I won't be at your side in this, despite what it means to me. I have to butt out."

"Since when do you help me, anyway? You know I do all your work for you, and you just step in at the end and get the credit."

He smiled, shook his head again, and spoke two words he normally didn't use in front of Velda.

"So you're in," Pat said.

"I'm in. Velda—any thoughts?"

She smiled at Pat and squeezed his hand; I thought he'd blush. "We can always use a dollar," she said.

Pat suddenly decided he was hungry after all and ordered a Reuben and fries. I went back to my knockwurst, but Velda had set what was left of her salad aside.

"Pat," she said, "Mike filled me in this morning, and there's a couple of things I don't understand."

Pat sipped his Pabst and nodded. "Go on."

"What's the motive in killing Chester Dunbar if all the kids stood to inherit equal shares?"

I answered for him. "Well, nobody inherits anything till you die, honey."

"But wasn't Chet Dunbar already quite elderly? Now, if one of the kids urgently needed money, maybe that would explain jump-starting the will. Otherwise, why not just let nature take its course?"

Pat said, "That's a good question, Velda. But I don't know the details of the will. I just know that Chet told me, long before he died, that he'd arranged for each of his heirs to receive equal shares."

Velda, thinking, said, "Is there some reason that all of them still live together in that house?"

He shrugged. "I have no idea. Living there is free, maybe?"

I said, "Maybe the will says that if you leave, you lose your interest in the house. That the last person living there inherits it. Just a guess."

"Maybe not a bad one," Pat said. "After all, there's no sign that their familial love is so strong they crave each other's constant companionship."

"Something else," Velda said, lifting a finger. "Let's say Chester Dunbar *was* murdered, possibly by one of his family to get a share of the will sooner than later. How would killing the butler figure in?"

I finished my Pabst and said, "This case is seriously screwed up. Whatever happened to 'the butler did it?' This time they did the butler."

Ignoring that, Pat said to Velda, "I think I can answer your question. This morning—before I had this matter yanked away from me—I spoke on the phone to Clarence Hines, of Hines & Carroll…"

"The family's law firm," I said.

Pat nodded. "Hines is the estate's executor. If you'll remember, Mike, the family attorneys were going to call on the Dunbars last evening. Why do you suppose that was?"

I shrugged. "I didn't give it a thought at the time, but come to think of it—why would the death of the family butler, accidental or otherwise, require the executor of the estate to drop by?"

"Because," Pat said, "Jamison Elder was to receive $250,000 upon his retirement at age seventy."

I gave a long low whistle. "That's a hell of a going-away present," I said. "Why seventy? That's well past retirement age."

"I don't know," Pat admitted. "I was able to get quite a bit out of Hines, who couldn't claim client confidentiality with his client dead and a possible homicide. But he did provide a possible murder motive for any one of the 'kids.'"

"What?" I asked.

Pat leaned in. "If Jamison died prior to age seventy, the money went back into the estate, or rather never left it. The Dunbars would get equal shares of that quarter million."

"That's over sixty grand a piece," I said.

"Sixty-two thousand five hundred," Velda said.

"That's a tempting figure."

"Thank you," she said.

Pat had said he'd call Dorena Dunbar and do his best to get the family's cooperation, though even without it, he still wanted me to proceed with the investigation. I was in the office at my desk waiting for Pat's call when Velda came in. She had a letter from the afternoon mail.

She had already opened it and took one last look before holding out the folded sheet to me, saying, "No return address. Monticello postmark."

"So it relates to Pat's case."

"Does it?"

I read the typed copy aloud. "'Coincidences are few and far between. I, too, have often wondered.'"

A small frown creased Velda's forehead as she sat sideways on the edge of my desk. "What do you make of it?"

"It's a letter designed to intrigue somebody who can think."

"Oh brother," she said. She gave me a gentle smirk and added, "So, Big Brain—enlighten me."

I ran my fingers over the letter deliberately, feeling the structure of the paper. After I'd done it twice, and her smirk was still there, I said, "Expensive stuff."

She nodded, waiting for a fuller explanation.

I gave her one: "You don't waste paper of this quality on a pointless mailing."

"What's it supposed to mean, then?"

"I'm thinking, kitten. Let's start with this—it isn't office stationery."

Her head went to one side as she shrugged, an arc of sleek black hair swinging. "Could be, if it came from a doctor. Or maybe a lawyer, or some sort of professional."

I grinned. "You're good, kiddo."

"So we're talking somebody important."

"And/or wealthy."

She nodded again. "And/or wealthy."

"Now, how about the contents?"

Her eyes widened, then narrowed. "Well, the writer is right. Coincidences *are* few and far between."

"*What* coincidence are we talking about, doll?"

"Writer's assuming you'd know."

"Should I?"

Her tongue ran over her lips while she thought about that. "Well, as I pointed out earlier, it was a coincidence that half a body washed up at your feet. But a bigger, more significant coincidence is that Chester Dunbar died accidentally, and now so has his butler."

I rustled the letter and asked her, "How about that last sentence?"

"What about it?"

"You like the commas?"

She took the thing back. "Somebody remembered his English usage. Now, who would *that* be?"

"How about somebody who teaches it?"

"Or studied it. Any other ideas, Mike?"

"Not yet. But Jamie Elder was British, and this letter has that sound."

"Well, he didn't write it from beyond the grave."

"So maybe his killer wrote it."

She frowned, no wrinkles. "Why, Mike?"

"To warn me, maybe."

"To warn you. Or... maybe to encourage you."

"To do what?"

"Somebody's telling you that Dunbar and Elder were murdered and it's no coincidence. And you should get involved."

"But it's ambiguous, doll. Could just as easily be warning me *not* to get involved."

"Or maybe... daring you to."

The phone rang and it was Pat. I held the phone so Velda could lean over and listen in.

"Dorena Dunbar will see you tonight," Pat said.

"Fine."

"At the house or mansion or whatever you want to call it. Eight o'clock. I figure you're going to stay in the area a while, so I made a reservation for you at Kutsher's."

That was one of the big Catskills resorts, just outside Monticello. With the rain beating at my window, I knew skiing was out and so was golf. Of course, neither one interested me.

I asked, "Who's in the showroom?"

"Henny Youngman."

We exchanged quick goodbyes and hung up.

Velda said, "So what does Dorena look like?"

"Oh, about sixty. Stubby gal. Thinning hair. Facial moles."

She smirked again. "You and Henny Youngman."

And here's what jumped into my mind: *Take my life, please.*

In the rain, the two-hour drive to the Dunbar mansion turned into three, though for the last half hour the wet stuff let up. Willie Walters, still in his ear-flap cap and hunter's plaid, was expecting me, opening the gates as soon as I pulled in. I gave him a wave and got one back, and guided my Ford Galaxie up the winding drive, which was made a glistening ivory by the three-quarter moon.

The slender Negro maid gave me an old-friends smile, took my hat and coat, and delivered directions down the hall to the library, where Dorena Dunbar was waiting. Along the way I heard typing, and I couldn't help but wonder if that machine was the one on which this afternoon's enigmatic note had been pounded out.

Like most big old houses anytime but summer, this one was on the chilly side, so it was no surprise to find Dorena in a beige cardigan and brown capri pants. Slender but shapely, the near-petite girl rose from a roll-top desk in a workspace notched into a wall of books. Every wall in here was books, mostly the leather-bound variety that were more for show than reading.

She came over and took my arm, apparently glad to see me, the full coral-lipsticked lips framing perfect white teeth in a smile that lightly crinkled the corners of the big brown Liz Taylor cat eyes. Her make-up was heavier than yesterday afternoon, but either way she had the kind of finely carved features that suggested either God in a good mood or a skilled plastic surgeon. At her age, probably the former, though you never knew.

"Mr. Hammer, I'm so pleased to see you," she said.

"Thank you," I said, though I almost asked, *Why?*

"Come and sit with me," she said, taking my hand and leading me to the middle of the room where, on an Oriental carpet worth some real money, brown-leather overstuffed couches faced each other across a low-slung coffee table.

But we didn't sit across from each other; instead,

she deposited me on the left-hand couch and settled in beside me, sitting with her back to the plump arm of the thing, a leg tucked under her. Very casual, and even familiar.

"I'm pleased you were willing to see me," I said.

"Pat... Captain Chambers... is an old family friend. I can't imagine any request from him that I'd turn down."

Lucky Pat.

She was leaning forward a little. "Oh, I'm sorry. I don't mean to be rude. Would you like something to drink? Coffee? A cocktail, perhaps? I wouldn't mind a glass of sherry myself."

"Four Roses and ginger?"

She bounced up. "Four Roses and ginger it is."

Her fanny was fun to watch as she swayed over to a well-stocked liquor cart in front of one of the walls of books.

As she poured, her back to me, weight on one leg, she asked, "How were the roads?"

"A little slick. Slowed me down some."

"That surprises me some."

"Why's that?"

"Your reputation... as a sort of reckless individual."

The little blonde turned with my drink in one hand and her own glass of sherry in the other. Her expression was faintly teasing and the big brown orbs bore a twinkle.

She handed me my drink and resumed her leg-tucked-under-her position, nestling in the niche between the armrest and the back cushion.

I glanced over at the roll-top desk, on which an electric typewriter sat like a plump gray Buddha. I said, keeping it light, trying not to seem rude, "You always do your correspondence this time of night?"

"Oh, that's not my correspondence. I'm working on my new play."

That implied previous ones.

Turning sideways to face her, I said, "I didn't know you were a playwright. That sounds ambitious."

She shrugged. "Well, a girl has to do something with her time."

"Isn't running this household enough? I assume that's what you do."

She nodded resignedly. "Yes, that's a responsibility I took on long ago. But we don't have a large staff. Just Lena the maid, Dixie the cook, some girls from town who clean, Willie the caretaker, and… well, there was Jamie, of course."

"Of course. Will you be hiring someone to take his place?"

"I don't know. We haven't got that far." Her bubbly mood was losing its fizz.

To help get her carbonated again, I asked, "So how did you get interested in writing plays? Have you had anything produced?"

She came bubbling back. "I did have something produced, last summer, at one of the Catskill playhouses. There's been interest from a producer about an off-Broadway staging, but that's still just so much talk."

"Impressive nonetheless." I gave her a kidding little smile. "What does a young woman like you have to write plays about?"

"Oh, dysfunctional families. Just like every playwright. How's the Four Roses and ginger? Did I get it right?"

"Perfect. Am I jumping the gun, Miss Dunbar, in assuming you approve or… anyway, sanction… the investigation Pat Chambers asked me to undertake?"

She nodded, saying, "I certainly am," adding, "and please make it Dorena."

"And I'm Mike. I have to say I'm a little surprised."

"Why is that, Mike?"

"Because I'll have to ask you and everyone around here plenty of embarrassing questions and go poking into uncomfortable areas."

She sipped the sherry. "Well, why don't you ask me something and we'll see if I get embarrassed or uncomfortable."

I suddenly had a hunch this wasn't her first sherry of the evening.

"Can you think of anyone," I asked, "who might have a motive for killing Jamison Elder?"

"No. He was a very nice man. He was like—"

"A member of the family?"

"Yes."

"Dysfunctional family or *Father Knows Best?*"

I was testing her a little, and she passed just fine: she smiled. Possibly a sherry-induced smile, but she smiled.

"Somewhere in between," she said.

"Did Jamison have a private life that you know anything about? I assume he had some time off."

She nodded. "He did. He had several evenings a week that were his own. For a while he was involved with a woman who taught high school, but she married someone else."

"When was this?"

"Twenty-some years ago. Daddy was still alive."

"No love life since then?"

A shrug. "Oh, he may have gone out with a female or two. He used to be active with his church. Episcopalian."

"Used to be?"

She nodded, sipped more sherry. "Yes, he lost interest or faith or something, maybe, oh… ten or twelve years ago?"

Was there nothing current in this man's life?

I asked, "Did he have any outside hobbies?"

"He played poker with some men his age, once or twice a month."

Finally a glimmer of something!

"Gambling, huh? Did he ever get in trouble over his losses?"

She shook her head. "I don't think so. I believe it was penny ante."

I was starting to think that Jamison Elder was already half-dead before he became half a corpse.

Bluntly, I said, "We need to talk about your father's death."

"Of course."

I shifted on the couch. "Then you agree with Pat that it might have been murder?"

She shrugged. "I always wondered."

"Can I see where it happened?"

There was nothing bubbly about her now. Her narrow pretty face turned white, the black make-up around her eyes and the coral coating of her lips giving her a kabuki look; but she nodded. She got up, left her sherry behind, and I did the same with my now-empty tumbler. I followed her to the high-ceilinged entry area and up the sweeping stairway to the second floor. Toward the end of the long hallway, at left, was her father's room.

For this having been the sleeping chamber of a very wealthy man, the effect was more like the cop he'd once been before inventing his way into big bucks. A double bed, nothing fancy, with a pair of nightstands. A dresser, no mirror. Across the room, a table with a comfy chair overseen by a standing lamp. The parquet floor had a few throw rugs, the walls some starving-artist landscape paintings.

The only thing vaguely rich-person about it was the private bath.

"Where was he found?" I asked her.

She stood by where that was, just outside the bathroom, and pointed down as if she'd just spotted the body for the first time.

"He had pills in there?" I asked.

She nodded.

I pointed across the room toward the table and comfy chair. "And there?"

She nodded.

I went over and had a look. A couple of fat bestsellers were on the reading table—*Hawaii, Advise and Consent.*

I asked, "He often read before he went to bed?"

"Yes."

"Didn't read in bed?"

"No, I don't think so."

Not a surprise—the low-wattage lamps on the nightstands didn't seem conducive to that.

"Do you recall," I asked, "which side of the bed he got out of that night? Which side of the covers had been disturbed?"

Her brow furrowed. "I think... I think the left side."

His right.

"And he kept some spare pills on the reading table, yet instead he came around and tried to make it to the bathroom, on the opposite side of the room."

"Does that mean something, Mike?"

"He may have gone to the reading table first, and found his pill bottle emptied... not by him... and wound up crawling toward the bathroom."

"And not making it," she said quietly.

"If he had," I said, "I doubt he'd have found any pills there, either."

"You mean… you *already* think it's murder?"

"It could be."

"But the police…?"

"They're good people, but lacking in imagination. Who found the body?"

"Jamison. When Father was late coming down for breakfast, he went up to check on him."

Maybe the butler did *do it*.

She'd been keeping it together well but seemed on the verge of coming apart, so I said, "I think we've spent enough time in here."

Before long we were back on the couch in the library. She got herself another sherry, and I had another Four Roses and ginger.

I asked, "Are your brothers here?"

"Stepbrothers. No. Well, my brother Chickie is, in his bedroom in the carriage house. But Dex and Wake go out most evenings."

"And this is no exception."

She nodded. "Madeline's out, too."

"With her husband?"

"Wake? Not hardly!"

"Are Wake and Dex together?"

"You do have a sense of humor, Mr. Hammer."

I sighed, sipped. "Well, that's too bad."

"What is?"

"I had hoped to talk to them. I'm pleased to have

your blessing to investigate, and that's probably enough… but I'd like to get the go-ahead from those two, as well."

Her eyebrows rose. "Oh, well… you have it."

"I do?"

She nodded and her blonde hair bounced. "They got on board right away. They're pleased to have you looking into Jamison's death, and Daddy's, too."

"Well… that surprises me."

"Why, Mike?"

"Meaning no offense, you and your brothers—"

"Stepbrothers."

"You and your stepbrothers are the only obvious suspects, if Jamison Elder's death was a homicide."

"We are?"

I nodded. "I'm aware, Dorena, that Elder's death pumps an extra sixty-some grand into each of your pockets."

She was looking past me, over the rim of the sherry glass. "I hadn't thought of that, but… I guess it's true." Then the big brown eyes fixed on me. "What's your daily rate, Mr. Hammer? Mike?"

"One-fifty a day plus expenses. But I already have a client."

"Who—Pat Chambers? Nonsense. He's your best friend. You won't charge him anything! Let the Dunbar family demonstrate to you that we welcome this investigation. That we welcome *you*, Mike. Where are you staying?"

"Kutsher's."

She waved that off. "Oh, that won't do. That's a madhouse. You'll stay right here with us!"

I argued some, on both points, but she was a forceful little thing when she wanted to be. I wound up with her as a client, and with a room in the mansion, till my investigation was done.

She put me in her father's room.

CHAPTER FOUR

Showered and shaved, and in suit and tie, I came down for breakfast just before eight a.m. and found two Dunbars seated at the big dining room table off the kitchen. Dexter was sitting toward the far end on the right, and Chickie at the far end on the left. Both kept the head-of-the-table chairs empty. Breakfast had apparently not yet been served.

The older Dunbar brother was in a charcoal mohair suit with a shades-of-gray silk tie. He might have been dressed to go off to a high-finance firm. Fittingly, he was reading a folded-open *Wall Street Journal* as he sipped his morning coffee.

Chickie was in a western-style gray shirt with a red embroidered yoke, a Lone Ranger patch on its red-trimmed breast pocket. He, too, had a paper open and was hunkered over doing a crossword puzzle.

Amazingly, it was the *New York Times*.

I said hello, getting a "Hi" from Chickie, who did not look up, and a "Mr. Hammer" from Dex, who gave me the barest glance and nod. Then I went on into the kitchen to see what the morning drill was.

The cook, Dixie, was a big friendly heavyset Negro woman right out of *Gone with the Wind*, only minus any Amos 'n' Andy accent. At the stove, after the introductions, she took my order, which I was told could be eggs any way I wanted and bacon with cottage fries. Orange juice if I liked, coffee already on the table.

"I'll bring it to you myself," she said, her cheerfulness taxed.

"Isn't cooking the meals enough?" I asked, kidding her a little after I'd made my requests. "Do you have to deliver 'em, too?"

"Used to be, Mr. Jamison did all that. He'd come up for breakfast and at supper, bringin' the boy along. For lunch, those two stayed over in the carriage house."

"Nice man, Mr. Jamison?"

"Nice man. Kindly man. At lunch, Lena helps out. It's a small staff, but there's only four who's livin' here."

"Four plus me, Miss Dixie," I said, grinning at her. "And I always bring my appetite."

She grinned back, cheerful again. "No problem, Mr. Mike."

"When does Miss Dunbar come down?"

"About an hour. Mr. Wake, he drags along 'bout ten."

"Not exactly a family that eats together."

"Supper, sometimes… but breakfast, no."

I was on my way back into the dining room when I paused and turned to ask her, "That boy Chickie… does he always do the *New York Times* crossword? I can't manage the one in *TV Guide*."

She shrugged big shoulders. "I know, it's the doggonedest thing. He's been doin' that, and good at it, long as I been here. Which is a good ten years anyway."

"Must be an idiot savant."

"Well, he's an idiot, all right."

I split the difference between Dex and Chickie, sitting halfway down on the former's side. Got myself some coffee, helped myself to the cream and sugar. Chickie, pausing for a sip from his glass of milk, met my eyes and smiled shyly, then returned to his crossword. The *Daily News* was on the table in case anybody was uncouth enough to be interested. I opened it to the funnies.

Breakfast was fine, the scrambled eggs not overcooked, the bacon nicely crisp, the potatoes tasty but not greasy. When I came into money, I'd hire Dixie away from these ungrateful slobs.

Dex stopped reading the *Journal* when his breakfast came—poached eggs and toast—but Chickie kept at the crossword when his food arrived, exactly the same order as mine. Great minds.

Between bites, I said to Dex, "I was pleased that you and your brother are okay with me looking into things."

He nodded, smiled faintly, but said nothing.

I went back to my eating.

"*Done!*" Chickie said, throwing down his pencil and raising his hands in triumph. Next to me, his stepbrother winced and maybe shuddered a little. Then Chickie bent over his breakfast and really dug in.

Dex finished before I did, and rose from his chair and seemed to be heading out until he stopped next to me, as if in afterthought, and said, "Could we talk sometime today, Mr. Hammer?"

With his dark hair and handsome oval face, he might have stepped out of an Arrow shirt ad.

"We'll have to, Mr. Dunbar. It's key that both you and your brother cooperate."

"Of course. I'm going down to my office in Monticello. Meet me there this morning. At your convenience."

He slipped his hand in his suitcoat pocket and handed me his business card with address:

Dexter J. Dunbar
Financial Services
312 Broadway Avenue
Monticello, New York

He'd really come prepared, unless he kept a stack of the things in his suitcoat pocket at all times.

When Dex had gone, Chickie suddenly said, "I walk over here by myself now."

"You do?"

The man/boy nodded. "Breakfast and supper. My

friend Mr. Elder used to walk me over, but he's in heaven now, you said."

"That's right. I'm sure you miss him. He was your teacher, wasn't he?"

Chickie nodded. "Maybe *you* could walk me back."

"Sure," I said.

We went outside through the library's French doors and, as we started down the fieldstone walk, Chickie slipped his hand in mine.

The air was crisp but not quite cold, the ground slushy, the snow existing only in occasional patches with some grass straggling through like a bald man's stubborn last strands. With the sun getting this ambitious, I wouldn't need the Burberry today.

"I miss Mr. Elder," Chickie said.

"I'll bet you do."

"Mr. Walters makes my lunch now."

"Does he?"

Chickie nodded. "Not as good as Mr. Elder, though. Just Campbell's soup. Sometimes spaghettiOs."

We were at the side door to the carriage house now. The little man let go of me, then turned with great formality and extended his hand for me to shake. I did. It wasn't much of a shake, but I appreciated the effort.

Then he went in and I headed back.

I pulled the Galaxie into a metered space just down from the Rialto Theater and just up from Rexall Drugs.

Monticello had a typical small-town business district, maybe more prosperous than most cities of 5,000 or so, with occasional indications—Kaplan's Hebrew National, the Bagel Bakery—that I was smack dab in the middle of the Borscht Belt.

There was nothing kosher about Dexter Dunbar's Financial Services. A storefront between a liquor store and a toy shop—something for everybody in downtown Monticello—the business sported an opaque plate-glass window whose greatest distinction was two spider-web-style, irregularly spaced bullet holes. The window was otherwise blank, although the steel-and-glass door to one side bore the "Financial Services" business name in gold-and-black script that tried a little too hard.

Soon I was entering into a drop-ceilinged, cheaply carpeted space with a few plastic molded chairs along the window wall, facing a vacant metal reception desk. A few decent framed paintings of Monticello landmarks—waterfall, ice caves, stone arch bridge—dressed it up a little. And somebody was keeping it clean, though a certain mustiness lingered. I flipped through the magazines on an end table by the chairs and didn't see anything less than a couple years old.

Dex appeared in the open doorway of his inner office, his expensive suitcoat off, his silk tie loose, looking like an Arrow ad only if it had been wadded up. He had a tumbler of reddish-brown liquid that might have been bourbon. It was ten o'clock in the morning.

"Get you something, Mr. Hammer?" he asked, hefting the tumbler.

He didn't look much like he was headed for Wall Street now, unless another Crash was coming and he was after a high window.

"No thanks," I said. "I usually wait till noon or so."

With his free hand he waved me to follow him, as he stepped back into his office.

This room was larger but just as empty—a metal desk with chair, a couple of file cabinets, no client chair. A black leather couch against one wall. Other than a phone, the desk was empty, not even a damn blotter; the suitcoat was slung over the back. A radio sat on one of the file cabinets. That was about it. Moving day with one small load left.

Since there was nowhere else for me to sit, he gestured to the couch, and I sat down. He joined me, sat turned sideways to face me. I leaned back with my arms along the rear cushions.

"Business has been slow," he said, by way of explanation.

I didn't let him get away with it. "You're not doing any business here. At least not any more. What happened?"

He wasn't drunk yet, but he was on his way in that loose, gentleman-drinker fashion that can be hard to spot. Seeing no sign of a liquor cart, I wondered if he had the bourbon under "B" in one of the file cabinets.

His smile was a rumpled thing that didn't remember

how to look embarrassed. "I did have a client list for a while. When my father was alive. But I gave some bad advice…" He shrugged, sipped, shrugged again. "…and turns out people just don't like losing money."

"But you still come down here? Every day?"

"Usually. I do have my investments to look after."

I didn't pursue that, instead saying, "Look, Mr. Dunbar—"

"Make it Dex. And I'll call you 'Mike,' okay?"

"Sure."

He sipped and smiled. "Everybody knows you, Mike. You're the famous Mike Hammer."

"I used to be. Dex, I need to ask you about your father's death, and about what happened to Jamison Elder."

Another shrug. "Why not?"

"Let's start with what may seem like ancient history. You were home the night your father died, weren't you? All night?"

He nodded. "From midnight on. But our rooms are at the other end of the hall. We heard nothing, not me or Wake or Dorena."

"What about Wake's wife?"

"Madeline was… away."

I wasn't sure what that meant, but that was better followed up with Madeline herself.

I asked, "No one ever looked in on your father, to make sure he was all right? He did have a heart condition."

Dex shook his head. "No one checked on Dad, not

on a regular basis. He made a point of being self-reliant. Anyway, with medication, he had it under control."

"It *would* have been if he'd got to his pills."

"Yes," Dex said with a frown. "I did wonder about that. I *do* wonder about that. There were pill bottles within fairly easy reach in two places."

"Right. His reading table and the bathroom counter."

Dex managed a sad expression. "The attack must have hit him hard and fast."

"The morning he was found, were there pills in both bottles?"

"Yes. Plenty."

"Did it occur to you, Dex, that maybe there weren't?"

He blinked. "Weren't what?"

"Pills in the bottles."

Shaking his head, he said, "No, Mr. Hammer, Mike… we checked. There were pills in both."

"But if there hadn't been, your father might have crawled to that reading table, found nothing, and tried to make it to the bathroom. Had he made it, I have a hunch that he wouldn't have found any help there either."

"I don't follow."

"I think someone emptied both bottles of pills, and then—after your father was dead—replaced them."

He squinted, as if trying to bring me into focus. "But that would mean…"

"Someone in the house did it. Yeah. And that limits the possibilities."

"You mean…the suspects."

I nodded. "It's down to you, your brother, his wife, your sister, your stepbrother, and the two live-in staff members, Jamison Elder and Willie Walters. Maybe the day staff, if they had keys, though I can't imagine what their motive might be."

He sat there thinking about that.

I got out a deck of Luckies and offered him one. He shook his head, his full attention on the subject at hand. And someone who drank that much had to work to do it.

Finally he said, "Jamison was who found the body, you know."

I lit up a Lucky, waved out the match. "I do know. Your sister told me. So what do you think, Dex? Who might have done it?"

Half a humorless smile appeared. "Well, I can rule *me* out even though you can't. Obviously, Wake and Dorena benefitted from Father's death, because it cleared the way for our inheritances."

"Does Chickie inherit anything?"

His shrug was dismissive even for a shrug. "The same as the rest of us, but it's tied up. Dorena will look after him, when the time comes."

"What if something happens to her?"

He shrugged again, but just one shoulder. "I don't know. Wake or me would look after him, I suppose. But she's the one who has a touch with the little moron. Sorry. That may have sounded a touch cruel."

A touch.

I asked, "How can a moron do the *Times* crossword?"

The question obviously bored him. "I don't know. There are things he's good at, and things where he's hopeless. Ask Dorena."

"Getting back to a murder motive, wouldn't Jamison Elder be a candidate? Finding the body, he was in a perfect position to re-fill those nitro bottles. And he had a quarter of a million in the will, right?"

"Oh, you know about that? Yes, he was in the will, but he had to work till seventy, taking care of Chickie, for that to kick in. And three years ago, when Elder was, what, sixty? Why would he choose then to get rid of an old man who was already in sketchy health?"

"Speaking of Jamison Elder, haven't you all benefitted from his death?"

His shrug this time was facial. "Sure, another sixty-some grand each got pumped into the family money pool. But none of us get anything till we're forty. Trust funds."

So that was why they were all living together in the mansion.

"If Elder, for whatever reason," I said, "killed your father, and one of you found out... revenge might be the motive."

"Are we even sure," Dex said, with a smirk, "that Elder was murdered? I hear the authorities are inclined to call it accidental."

"That's what I've been hired to determine," I said,

letting out some smoke. "Anyway, the authorities sometimes take the easiest route."

"Well, old Jamison didn't, plowing into that snow bank." His glass was empty, and he got up. "Are you sure I can't get you anything, Mike?"

"No, I'm fine."

He went over to the file cabinets, opened the top drawer of one and got out a bottle of Jim Beam Single Barrel. Thought so. He poured himself some and came back over and sat again.

His expression turned chummy. "Listen, Mike, I agreed to talk to you… in fact, agreed to go along with your investigation, even when I don't think there's anything to investigate… because I have a little matter of my own I could use some help with."

"That right?"

"Oh yes." He sipped, savored, swallowed. "Is my sister paying you enough, or would I have to kick in something extra to get your help?"

"Run it by me and we'll see."

"It's just… I'm a little short right now. In fact, that's the problem."

"You can owe me, if need be."

"I'd rather not owe anybody anything. That *is* the problem!" He sat forward, his eyes sober, even if he wasn't. "Mike… have you ever heard of a slimy weasel called Abe Hazard?"

I nodded. "Fat little hood who used to run smalltime gambling operations for Luciano in Queens and the Bronx. Floating crap games, mostly. Why, is he still alive?"

"All too. He has this establishment, a rather nice one actually, called the Log Cabin. It's in the countryside, in a lovely wooded area, providing easy access to the folks staying at the various Catskills resorts. The law stays away from him. The idea is, he's not hurting anyone, and this is a vacation area, and why not let the visiting yokels have a good time."

"Don't tell me. You've been having a good time, too."

He sighed. Deep. "Not lately. I've hit a streak of bad luck."

"How long has it lasted?"

"About… three years."

Since his stepfather died, I'd bet. If I were a betting man. But it was a safe one that Daddy hadn't put up with Sonny Boy's drinking and gambling. Another motive?

He spoke softly, as if someone in the otherwise empty office might hear. "I'm into Hazard for a goodly sum…"

"How goodly?"

"Just over one-hundred grand."

"Damn."

He made a defensive face. "Well, it was gradual. I'm not some dope who gambles tens of thousands at a go."

"No, I'm sure you aren't. You probably lost a thousand or so at a time."

"That's right. Sometimes only hundreds. Well, Abe ran me a line of credit for a long time, and then recently he hit me up for what I owe. He knew, I'd already *told* him, in clear plain English, that until I turned forty, I wouldn't have that kind of money. He'd have to cover me till then. And, before, he always said he would!"

"But he's changed his mind?"

"I don't know. I think so. He hasn't exactly said."

I frowned. "Well, then, why—"

"He told me he wanted me to sign something that turned half of my inheritance over to him. Half! And for no further line of credit. He says I should consider it interest on the one-hundred grand."

"He's probably getting pressured by whoever he works for to balance the books. Likely he's controlled by the Evello crowd back in the city."

Dex almost whispered now: "Did you... did you happen to see those bullet holes out front?"

"I noticed."

"Few days ago, somebody across the street, from behind a parked car, *shot* at me! It echoed off the pavement like goddamn thunder! Whether it was to scare me or... or *kill* me, I don't know."

I grunted a laugh. "Ever hear of the Golden Goose? Killing you makes no sense."

"Not necessarily. Hazard might be able to hit the estate up for what I'm into him for. He's got it in writing."

This guy.

I asked, "Did you call the police?"

"No. It was late, nobody around. I'd been sleeping one off here on the couch, and it was, oh, maybe midnight. There aren't any bars on this block, so nobody was around. I didn't figure going to the cops was a good option."

"Maybe not. What do you want me to do about it?"

"See if it is Hazard who made that attempt on me, or made it happen."

"You staying away from there?"

Now he finally got embarrassed. "No. I'm not totally broke. I have an income. And the Log Cabin's the only casino around."

"Well, a man has to have his fun."

He put his hand on my coat sleeve. "Look. You're Mike Hammer."

"That's the rumor."

"If you... what's the word? Roust him? Maybe Abe'll back off. Or maybe you can get him to admit he did it or had it done, or even convince you he didn't. Of course, he has some bullyboys you may have to wade through. What do you say?"

"I think I'll have a glass of that Jim Beam," I said.

When I got back to the Dunbar place, I found Dorena in the library again, waling away at her typewriter. With her chin-length hair back in a cute stubby ponytail, and wearing a light blue turtleneck pullover and navy stretch pants, she looked very collegiate. She didn't hear me come in—no doors to these main downstairs rooms—so I waited till she got to a stopping place.

"How go the Broadway wars?" I asked.

She turned in her swivel desk chair to smile at me. Her make-up was light, no Cleopatra eyes, but the lips glowed coral.

"Lillian Hellman has nothing to worry about, I'm afraid," she said. "But a girl has to try."

"Hey, it worked for Agatha Christie. I never saw that *Witness for the Prosecution* twist coming."

That made her smile even more. "Maybe I'll try a mystery next. Do you need something from me?"

She put it sweetly, but I was interrupting.

"No," I said, "I just wondered if your brother Wake was around. Or did he finally get around to going in to the city to identify Jamison Elder's body?"

Half of it, anyway.

"Oh," she said, "Wake didn't have to go in. Pat called and said the sister was coming in from Delaware to do that, and make arrangements for the return of the, uh…"

"Her brother's remains, yeah. So is Wake around, then? I need to talk to him."

She made a little face. "He's where he always is, when he's not off gallivanting. His studio."

"Where's that?"

She pointed vaguely. "It's over the garage. He fixed it up special for himself, after Daddy died. Before that he just painted out on the back porch."

"How does he feel about being disturbed?"

"Who cares? The side door into the garage will be unlocked. You'll find pull-down stairs at the back up to the studio."

"Thanks, kid."

Her mouth twisted prettily. "You make me sound so young."

"Is that a bad thing?"

Her answer was a smirk and she returned to her typing as I went out.

The four-car garage boasted quite an automotive array: a white Jaguar, vintage '56 or so, already a classic; a dark blue Lincoln; a red Thunderbird; and a dark green Triumph TR4. The detective in me couldn't help making deductions—the Jag would be Wake's, the Lincoln Dex's, the Thunderbird Dorena's, and the Triumph Madeline's. The latter might be a little small for the long-legged gal, but green flattered redheads, so that one was hers.

But I must be wrong about the Lincoln, because Dex was presumably still at Financial Services back in Monticello, and he'd had to get there somehow. I shrugged to myself.

At the back of the neatly kept garage, I pulled down collapsible wooden stairs up to what had been a loft before Wake made a studio out of it. The steps were old white-washed wood, though the third-from-the-top one was unpainted fresh pine.

I emerged into an impressive space whose north-side glass wall rose to a skylight.

"That would be Mr. Hammer, I'd wager," Wake said.

He was seated at a medium-sized canvas, his back to me, in a paint-spattered smock and chinos.

I said, "I thought your brother was the betting man in the family."

"Odds are he is."

I immediately recognized the painting in progress as nearly identical to that of the stone arch bridge I'd seen on a wall of his brother's dreary reception area. Craning around, I noticed several twins of the current painting leaned against the non-glass walls as well as multiples of the other two I'd seen at Financial Services, a waterfall and ice caves. Several other Monticello landmarks were represented, including the local synagogue and Kutsher's (where I'd almost stayed) in all its neon glory.

These representational paintings were very good, but what struck me were their companions—much larger canvases that were a kind of modern art variation on Impressionism. At first glance they seemed abstract, geometric shapes, but on closer look they took form, and figures could be discerned.

"You're good," I told him, at his side.

"Thanks." He still didn't look at me. "Which do you dig? The corn-ball landscapes or the way-out stuff?"

"Let's just say," I said, "the ones that make me go, 'Crazy, man, crazy.'"

"Ah. You sound like a relic of the Beatnik days, my friend."

"I'm a relic of further back than that."

He put his palette on the worktable beside him and finally met my eyes. He looked a lot like a blond version of his brother, but the handsome features had a delicacy that Dex lacked.

"I bet you have questions for me," he said, wiping his hands with a rag smelling of turpentine. He was much more pleasant than he'd been the other night. "Shall we sit?"

He gestured to a low-slung couch whose sparkly upholstery spoke of an earlier decade, and whose threadbare cushions said secondhand. Perfect for a studio like this.

The artist crawled out of the smock and flung it carelessly onto a plank floor that might have been a Jackson Pollock painting, exposing a light blue work shirt with its sleeves rolled up. The ankles of the chinos were paint-spattered, but not to the degree of the smock.

I sat, and he was about to, when he stopped and said, "You look like you could use a beer."

I grinned at him. "I could. I almost let your brother talk me into some Jim Beam, but I came to my senses."

He went over to a nearby cooler and got out two cans of Pabst, used a churchkey on them, and handed me mine. He settled in next to me, sipping, leaving the center cushion open. Relaxing, a leg over a knee, glad to take a break.

"My brother is a lush, Mr. Hammer. Isn't that a wonderful word? Lush. The dictionary meaning is 'rich.'"

"I think that's a different lush."

"Are you sure? Plenty of rich people qualify. So. I know you have questions to ask about my stepfather and the late Mr. Elder. What would you think about a painting in tribute to friend Jamison? An overhead view of an ice block afloat with something on it that might be half a man? They'd study that one in the Village, that's for damn sure."

I gestured to the canvases leaned against the wall on either side of the couch. "Is that where the real paintings go? To the Village?"

He nodded. "I have a wall of them in a Houston Street gallery. Go for thousands, when they sell."

"Do they? Sell?"

"Not frequently, but you know the story about the lover boy who asks every good-looking girl he sees if he can screw her. Ninety-nine say no, but oh that hundredth."

I gave that the chuckle it was worth. "What do the landscapes go for?"

"A couple hundred each. I have a gallery, all mine, in Monticello, on Broadway. They do well. So what can I tell you about dear dead Daddy and our late lamented butler?"

I asked him the same questions as his brother, and his answers were very similar, without sounding rehearsed. He said if his stepfather was killed, he agreed that somebody in the house would have to have done it.

"But nobody immediately benefitted," he said, shaking his head, frowning. "Stepdad was in poor health. He'd have run out of gas on his own before very long. And as Dex may have told you, the four of us have trust funds. With Daddy alive or dead, we get access to those at forty. That's when life begins, they say."

"So I hear. I'll know soon enough."

We toasted beer cans.

"Now I have another question," I said.

"Shoot. Whoa, not a smart thing to say to Mike Hammer. But shoot."

"Okay. Why are you so goddamn cooperative?"

"Well…" His grin was of the shit-eating variety. "…I have a favor to ask of you. No, that's wrong. I can afford to pay you. But this is a perfect situation for me."

"It is?"

He nodded. "With you here—working for Dorena, investigating two deaths that I personally think are accidental—you can do a job for me without raising any suspicion."

"What job would that be?"

He waved the question off. "Let me give you a little background first. You met Madeline, my lovely wife?"

"Yes, briefly. And she is lovely. You're a lucky man."

"You don't know *how* lucky. And, Mr. Hammer…"

"Mike," I corrected.

"Mike… when you say Madeline is lovely, what you mean is, she's one incredible piece of ass."

"I generally don't say as much to the husbands."

He grunted a laugh. "Well, she is. She's fantastic. And plenty of guys agree with me. She's out almost every night with such admirers. Giving it away. Flaunting it. If she were discreet, I wouldn't mind so much. I've asked her to curtail her extracurricular activities, and she just laughs at me. Lately I've been talking divorce, and ugly though it might be, embarrassing as it would be for the Dunbars, what she's been doing would be ludicrously easy to prove."

I put up a hand. "Let me stop you there, Wake. I don't do divorce work. Not my specialty, not my deal."

He sat forward and, with his free hand, touched my arm. "No, you misunderstand. I tell you all of this strictly by way of background."

"Well… okay…"

He gulped some beer, belched, said, "We have a prenup that states Mad gets nothing from me until my trust fund kicks in. If I divorce her, with the endless list of correspondents she's racked up? She'll get little or no alimony."

"I follow," I said, and was starting to.

He gestured toward the hole in the floor where the steps emptied out, attic-style. "Did you happen to notice the one new slat in the stairs?"

I nodded. "About three down."

"What's below it?"

"Cement."

"What might a fall like that do to a person?"

"Break his damn neck."

He nodded in smiling agreement. "Well, that new slat replaces one that broke on me. But I caught myself and don't seem to be dead."

"Was the broken slat sawed to make that happen?"

"Not apparently. It was a rough break, jagged. I would guess pre-broken and then fitted back together. Understand, Mike, that no one comes up here but me. The studio is strictly off limits when I'm working."

I was proof that this wasn't entirely accurate, but I didn't comment.

He said, "Did you happen to notice the white '56 Jag below?"

I'd gotten that one right. "Oh yeah. A honey. Who belongs to the Lincoln, by the way?

"Dex. It's his boring style."

I frowned. "How'd he get into the office this morning, then? Hitchhike?"

He smirked. "Dexie's latest chippie probably picked him up. My brother's had a succession of 'em, sometimes more than one at a time, sniffing around the money he'll come into, before they lose interest and get tired of waiting. They usually chauffeur him home, too, because at the end of his 'work' day, he's frequently a little too lubricated to drive."

That had me thinking. "Any of these women married?"

"I believe the latest one, Brenda Something, *used* to be. Why?"

Somebody besides Abe Hazard might want Dex dead.

"No reason," I said. I'd got him off track, so I steered him back on course. "You mentioned your Jag—a real beauty."

"Yes, it is. Of course it's getting a little long in the tooth. I almost had a very bad accident last week, y'know."

"Oh?"

He shrugged, but it was feigned casualness. "I'm afraid I've been known to break the speed limit from time to time. Well, almost *all* the time. I have to make many, many trips into the city, to the Village, and it's two hours within the law. Traffic allowing, *I* can make it in eighty minutes. And of course some of these roads wind around awfully... some are even mountainous."

"Your brakes went."

His grin was a bitter thing. "All at once. After the Jag got towed into the shop, I learned that the brake hose had a hole deep enough so that the thing would hold, under moderate braking... but give way with heavy braking."

"It was clearly cut?"

He shook his head. "No. The brake hose was old and needed replacing... but someone may have helped a possible hole reach its full potential, shall we say."

"And you didn't report either this incident or the

broken step, knowing they'd be written off as accidents."

He finished his beer, belched again. "Correct. Now, getting back to the little woman… if a woman with legs that long might be termed little… there's *one* way she might get around our prenup."

"If you were to die," I said.

He smiled. "If I were to die."

CHAPTER FIVE

Half an hour past Monticello, outside the town of Montgomery, I pulled into the chain-link fenced-off parking lot of the low-slung fieldstone building labeled NEW YORK STATE POLICE. With the sun really taking it out on the remaining snow, I wore my sunglasses to ward off the reflectiveness.

A figure in the gray woolen uniform and tan, purple-banded Stetson hat of the State Police was leaning against a black-and-white patrol car near the building, smoking a cigarette. He was wearing sunglasses too, a big man, as big as me, with a square jaw and Apache cheekbones, and somehow his very casualness said, "Don't mess with me."

This had to be Corporal Jim Sheridan, who I'd spoken to on the phone, arranging a meeting.

I pulled into one of the VISITORS stalls in front of

the building and took the short walk over to him. We introduced ourselves, went through the handshake ritual, and I lighted one up while he pitched his away.

"I thought, Mr. Hammer, that you might like to see the scene of the accident."

Not "scene of the crime."

"Makes sense," I said. "Call me Mike, and is Jim okay or do you prefer Corporal?"

A shy smile flickered on a craggily, almost-handsome face. "With no one else around, make it Jim. I kind of feel like I know you."

"Well, you're a friend of Pat's. I come with the package. You've worked a couple of shared investigations, I hear."

"Yup, but we really got to know each other at police conventions around the country. Still waters run deep with that guy."

"They do, but it's usually branch water."

He chuckled and got in behind the wheel. I came around and climbed into the rider's seat.

"I get the feeling," I said, "that you don't make the Jamison Elder death a murder."

He started up the engine; it had a throaty hum. "I can't honestly say I have an opinion... certainly not one that might clash with the Orange County coroner's."

I frowned. "Has there been an inquest already?"

"There won't be one. That's purely at the coroner's discretion, and he labels Elder an accident."

"Does your nose agree with it?"

"It doesn't disagree. We'll be there in half an hour and you can form your own opinion."

We were out of the parking lot now, and on the road.

I said, "You've talked to Pat about this, right?"

He nodded. "And it seems to me his suspicions grow mostly out of misgivings about that *other* accidental death—Chester Dunbar. Mike, I'll tell you what I told Pat—I'm just not familiar with that case."

"*Was* it a case?"

"Well, not really. The trooper who covered—what the record says was—Dunbar's accidental death chose at the time *not* to call in the B.C.I."

The Bureau of Criminal Investigations was the plainclothes branch of the State Police that responded to situations called to their attention by uniformed men like Sheridan. Troopers handled assault and larceny and malicious mischief, but not murder.

"What if I come up with new evidence?" I asked, and shared my thoughts about the two pill bottles that may have been emptied and then refilled, and not by a pharmacist.

He glanced at me, rays glinting off the sunglasses. "That's not evidence, Mike. It's a theory. And it's a theory about a three-year-old closed case."

There might have been a hint of sneer in my smile. "See, even you can't call it anything but a 'case.' Where I come from, there's no statute of limitations on murder."

I'd let a little edge into my voice, and he glanced at

me with a world-weary smile, eyes hidden behind the dark lenses.

"Mike, I know all about you. I even envy the short-cuts to justice you can take that somebody like me mustn't. Pat says you have a nose that can sniff out murder like nobody else. So if you turn something up, by all means I'll take it seriously."

"Thanks."

An eyebrow rose above the sunglasses. "Now that's not carte blanche to do as you please, understand. The way we're overworked, as shorthanded as we are, I'm happy to have you sniffing around two accidental deaths that might be a little too convenient."

I would like to have told him about the possible murder attempts on Dex and Wake Dunbar. But as my clients, they'd been pledged confidentiality. Still, I knew damn well their respective assumptions about who was out to kill them—Abe Hazard and Madeline Dunbar respectively—might be dead wrong. Someone might be trying to increase the estate's money pot. Someone like sweet Dorena, for instance, or either one of the two brothers, if one was lying to me about murder attempts. Even supposedly harmless Chickie, who also stood to gain.

I stabbed out the butt in the ashtray and asked, "Why are you so overworked? It's still the off-season, isn't it? For a while yet?"

"Catskills aren't what they used to be," the trooper said, both hands on the wheel. Traffic outside

Montgomery was a little heavy. "But the tourist trade is still a year-round thing. You might even be able to get some skiing in."

"No thanks. My idea of exercise is chasing my secretary around the office."

"Ha. What's hers?"

"Chasing me when I get winded." I lighted up another Lucky. "Jim, if you don't want to tell me what's giving you troopers heartburn, I understand."

He gave me a quick grin that was an admission that he'd been ducking my question. Then the grin faded as quickly as it came.

"We've had another missing girl," he said.

"Another?"

He nodded. "Number eight over the past couple of years."

"Runaways?"

His headshake was barely perceptible. "That's the thing—they're all of age. Eighteen to twenty-two. They've been vacationing on their own till this last one. You know, spring breaks and that kind of thing. One was a secretary from the city on her week off."

"And since they're of age, they might just have taken off somewhere because they felt like it."

Half a humorless smile carved itself in a craggy cheek. "In this latest instance, the girl was vacationing with her parents... but was eighteen. And they were overbearing types. You know how over-protective a Jewish mother can be."

"I know how over-protective an *Irish* mother can be. So the current missing girl looks like maybe an of-age runaway."

"She does." His sigh rattled out of his chest. "The only lead we have is a guy about five eight, broad-shouldered, seen chatting up this latest girl in the parking lot at the All-Night Room at the Concord resort, outside Monticello. Or anyway we think it's the same guy—descriptions tally."

"It's a start."

"Well, you can bet we're taking this seriously."

"Why the troopers? Why not the B.C.I.?"

The blank lenses swung momentarily my way. "These aren't murders, Mike. Not that we know of, anyway. And these little towns, even the bigger ones like Monticello, don't have police departments with the capacity to do missing persons investigations. And no state lines have been crossed to our knowledge, and anyway we have no bodies, so the FBI aren't in it. We've had some support from the local paper. But it feels tragic. It *smells* tragic."

"Now who has the nose for murder?"

He grunted something that was almost a laugh. "*This* is the case I'd like your help on, Mike."

"I wouldn't mind giving it. But if some sick prick is killing these girls, I can't promise I'd call you before I did something about it."

"Like blow the bastard away with that fabled .45 of yours?"

"If I couldn't think of something more fun." I sat up. "Say—something just occurred to me… what car was Elder driving?"

There had been four vehicles in the four-car garage, and the car the butler had driven was still impounded.

The trooper said, "One of those woody station wagons. '61 Country Squire. The family lets the help use it sometimes, I'm told, to go buy groceries and pick up cleaning and such. But it belongs to Wake Dunbar, who uses it to pack up his artist's gear for when he wants to go out and paint in the great outdoors."

"He did seem anxious nothing had happened to it, and that he'd get it back."

"He will, soon enough."

The drive along the country road was so scenic it might have been a worthy subject for an artist like Wake—plush tall pines touched with clumps of snow holding out against the spring thaw, occasional non-firs standing skeletal like ghosts haunting the woods.

Finally we approached a rustic, almost ramshackle covered bridge, its blistered wood gray with age, its peaked roof like a wounded soldier's proud cap. The ground fell somewhat steeply on either side, the stream the bridge crossed interrupting a gentle hillside. Chunks of ice still floated, making their way to the Hudson, but none were floes big enough now to carry even half a body.

Corporal Sheridan pulled over and we got out. The ground was soft and still clotted with snow. We walked across the narrow macadam road, and the trooper pointed at muddy tire-tread gouges in the shrinking snowbank.

"Elder must have caught a patch of ice," Sheridan said, "and plowed in here."

"Were there skid marks?"

"No, but with black ice, you don't always have them. And there was still enough snow the night it happened to stop him. The coroner thinks Elder hit his head on impact, on the steering wheel, where considerable blood of his type was found. That's consistent with his head wound."

"What about the idea that some other driver came along and hit him after he locked and walked away from that Country Squire?"

"That's a possibility." The trooper turned and pointed to the one-lane bridge. "Elder must have stumbled out of the car and walked across the bridge toward Bear Mountain Bridge, where he could phone for help. This road curves around and hugs the embankment. A dark night, stumbling around maybe in the middle of the road, poor guy might've been clipped by another driver and gone rolling down into the stream and, well, you know the rest."

I pitched what was left of my Lucky into the stream. "You're asking me to believe he *fell* onto that chunk of ice? That nobody put him there to die of loss of blood and exposure?"

"It's possible."

"Let's say you're right, Jim. And that Rube Goldberg of a death went down just that way. If it's hit-and-run, it's homicide. Call in the B.C.I."

He shook his head. "Stunned and staggering, Elder could have lost his equilibrium, passed out, rolled down into the cold water. All on his own. He might've been hit by a car, yes, but there were no signs of it on the body."

"Hell, man, there was only *half* a body!"

Sheridan looked at me with mild frustration, but not quite irritation. "So what's your scenario?"

I pointed down the road, away from the bridge, the direction we'd come. "Suppose somebody roared up behind him, flashing their lights. He recognizes the car as someone he knows and pulls over. The driver comes up, and Elder rolls the window down, and this familiar party smashes the old boy's head into the steering wheel. Then he hauls the butler's unconscious body out of the car and drags it down to the stream and, possibly with an accomplice, tosses him onto an ice floe. Then somebody drives the Country Squire into the snowbank."

"That's a little elaborate, isn't it?"

"Not any more than your staggering accident victim who somehow flips himself onto that chunk of ice like Little Eva fleeing Simon Legree. You said Pat told you I could smell murder. Don't *you*? It stinks! A secluded road, little traveled that time of night. Imagine two men, one grabbing Elder by the arms, the other by the legs, just tossing his dazed ass into the ice-choked river and onto that floe. A murder without quite killing the guy. Letting the cold and river and blood loss do it for them. Isn't that possible?"

Sheridan didn't say anything for a long time. Then he said, "Maybe."

"As in, maybe you should call in the B.C.I.?"

"Maybe as in maybe."

I put a friendly hand on his shoulder and stared into the lenses at my own crazed reflection.

"Fine," I said. "But if I catch up with whoever did this nasty thing before you decide you're interested? I'll make sure to show them less mercy than they gave to Jamison Elder."

He nodded somberly. "And I'll make sure to pretend you didn't say that."

The diner—off Route 17 on the way to the Monticello raceway, a year-round harness racing track—was one of those aluminum boxcars they built before the war, back when the Space Age was Buck Rogers not Sputnik. It was late afternoon, not yet suppertime, and I was here to meet Clarence Hines of the law firm Hines & Carroll.

Jukebox rock 'n' roll was going, not so loud as to be obnoxious. The joint's interior was black-trimmed chrome and turquoise vinyl, the counter stools mostly vacant this time of day, the blowsy blonde waitress behind it looking bored.

Most of the booths were empty, too, but at the far end a fiftyish-looking character leaned out, gestured with a coffee cup in hand, and cheerfully called out, "Mr. Hammer! Back here."

I went down and slid in opposite him in a high-backed booth, tossing my hat on the table. He had what must have been a sturdy frame before time and pie—he was halfway through a piece of coconut crème—caught up with him. His charcoal worsted would have been too good for the place if it hadn't looked slept in. The black-and-white silk tie seemed fresh enough.

"Thanks for meeting me here, Mr. Hammer."

No handshake.

"Thanks for seeing me, Mr. Hines."

His salt-and-pepper hair had the look of a ten-dollar haircut that could use a nickel comb dragged through it, and his mustache was a gray fringe over a smile that was too wide by half. His mildly bloodshot gray eyes had the sort of droopy lids that whispered drink or exhaustion or both.

"I had a house closing in this part of the world," he said, in a courtroom baritone toned down for indoors, "so I thought this might make a convenient meeting place. Would you like a piece of pie? It's excellent. Homemade."

Not unless whoever baked it slept somewhere behind the food slot it wasn't.

"Ah, Debbie!" he said, looking up at the bored blonde waitress who had selflessly made the trek over here from behind the counter. "Give this gentleman whatever he wants."

"Coffee," I said. "Milk not cream, sugar."

"You callin' me 'sugar,' big boy, or do you want it in your coffee?"

"Sugar, sugar."

She nodded and trudged off, like a native bearer on a safari.

I said to the attorney, "I have a hunch you didn't want to meet in your office for some reason other than a house closing."

He had a bite of pie, washed it down with coffee, and said, "You've caught me. It's my partner—Leo. The Carroll in Hines & Carroll? He's rather a stickler for legalities."

"I guess that could be a drawback in a lawyer."

He laughed at that, a little too much. "Leo would have wanted something in writing from all the Dunbars, with the exception of Charles of course, before talking with you. But getting a call from Dorena, asking for me to be frank with you, was good enough for me. Wonderful girl, Dorena."

"Yeah, I like her. I already know Dorena and her stepbrothers don't get their dough till they turn forty."

He nodded. His face looked soft, like wax getting ready to melt. "Dex is thirty-six, and Wake thirty-five. So they are, you might say, within spitting distance of their fortunes. As for Dorena, she's twenty-eight, so she has some way to go."

"What about Chickie?"

"Charles? Well, he's twenty and, because of his, uh, unusual status, shall we say, he has the longest wait of all... and even then, Dorena will control his funds."

"I take it you're the executor of the estate, Mr. Hines."

My coffee came. I thanked Debbie, calling her "Sugar" again, and she tried to work up a flirtatious smile that only came off sullen. But the coffee was good.

Hines said, "I am indeed the executor, but Dorena is Charles' legal guardian. Chickie, as the family calls him, is a... special case. Still... there are areas where he has made strides."

"I saw him do the *New York Times* crossword today easier than I do the Jumble."

Hines laughed lightly. Finished with his pie, he slid the plate aside. "Chickie has areas where he is normal or even shines—vocabulary is one. He reads fairly voraciously, although his literary tastes run to the Hardy Boys and Tom Swift."

"Where else does he shine?"

He thought about that, then said, "Reading is about the extent of it. Abstract concepts elude him, I'm afraid, and he has difficulty communicating. I do think Mr. Elder did amazing things with the boy—he home-schooled Chickie, you know."

I sipped coffee. "Chester Dunbar seems to have really kept Chickie under wraps. Wouldn't it've been better to get the boy professional help?"

The soft face conjured a rumpled smile. "Who are we to judge, Mr. Hammer, how a father chooses to raise a son? I knew Chet well enough to tell you, frankly, that he loved Chickie very much… but that he was tortured by the tragedy of so… so stunted an offspring."

"I'm no psychologist, but what little I've seen of the boy suggests autism. And that might be better dealt with in ways other than just locking him away in a carriage house."

Debbie came and refilled the lawyer's coffee and left. Hines sipped it, not commenting on what I'd just said, but those droopy gray eyes were shifting with thought.

"Is there something you're not telling me, Mr. Hines?"

"…I am not sure I should be getting into this. Even with Miss Dunbar's blessing, some of the details of the will would seem better left to the executor and the family members."

"Not when the family members have hired an investigator to look into two possible murders."

"The authorities consider both deaths accidental."

"But my clients don't. And they're your clients, too, Hines. Spill it."

He huffed a laugh. "Ah, the tough patois of the street tough. You live up to your reputation as something of a brute, Mr. Hammer."

"Oh, I haven't even started yet."

He studied me, wondering if I was the type who would shake the truth out of a person. What do you think?

Then, rather stiffly, he said, "To my knowledge, no

medical professionals have ever examined Charles."

"That's nuts."

Another shrug. "Perhaps. But that was how Chester Dunbar chose to deal with his son's disabilities. It's quite possible Dorena, as Chickie's legal guardian, may do otherwise."

"She hasn't in the three years since her father died."

"That's true. But one day she will." He seemed to catch himself. Had he said too much? "Are you sure you won't have a slice of pie? I'm considering having another, self-indulgent though that might be."

"I don't want pie, Mr. Hines. I want answers. What do you mean, 'one day she will?'"

He fought with himself, then finally said, "At age forty, Charles will be examined by medical professionals."

I leaned forward. "This is one of the terms of the will? That was Chester Dunbar's wish?"

"Yes."

"Hell, it's a little late to bring the medics in, isn't it? Age *forty?*"

He flipped a hand. "Again, your judgment and mine of Chester Dunbar's decisions matters not a whit. His wishes live on, in the terms of his last will and testament. And I, as executor of the estate, must honor those wishes. Just as you must do your clients' bidding."

"What's the purpose of a mandatory examination of a forty-year-old 'boy?'"

Again, the attorney seemed ill at ease. He might

have been on the witness stand while I, a dogged prosecutor, bore down on him.

"Mr. Hammer, if Charles passes muster, shall we say, under such an examination, he will get his share of the estate. The final trust-fund money will be turned over to him."

"And if he doesn't?"

"Dorena Dunbar will control those funds."

I frowned. "With what restrictions?"

"None. Her father trusted his daughter implicitly."

I didn't know what to make of that.

"Every five years," he added, "Charles will be tested again. Until the day he dies."

I said, "What kind of money are we talking here, counselor? I know Chester Dunbar was rich, from that wartime invention of his…"

"Oh, that was not his only success, Mr. Hammer. Until it burned down some, oh, dozen years or so ago, he had a workshop in Monticello, and from there came some wonderful, and profitable, inventions. For instance, working on a prototype for a heart rhythm recording device, he somewhat accidentally developed the first pacemaker. Trying to invent a wallpaper cleaner, he stumbled onto a non-toxic modeling clay… which is that colorful stuff now familiar to every schoolchild and parent."

"Okay, he had a knack, particularly for stumbling onto things. So what kind of money do these trust funds hold?"

A deep breath in and out. "Both stepsons and Dorena... and Charles, if he's deemed fit at forty to handle his own finances and, well, his own life... will receive in excess of one million dollars."

I let out a low whistle. "A cool million each?"

"A very cool million each, Mr. Hammer... more, now that the money Jamison Elder would have received will be plowed back into the estate."

No wonder there was murder in the air.

"Okay," I said, "but there are a few things that don't add up to me. Why reward Jamison Elder so generously? How does a butler rate like that?"

"Oh, he's not alone. William Walters will receive $250,000 upon his retirement at age sixty-five."

"Why the hell?"

"Chester Dunbar came to realize that these two individuals were, well, *good* with Charles. They could handle him, and were patient with him, and in their own way even loved the boy."

"He's a man now, counselor."

"I beg to differ, Mr. Hammer. Charles remains a child. And as for making Elder and Walters beneficiaries—even if it took some time for that to take effect—Chester Dunbar wanted to ensure that his son would be well taken care of after his death. Between Dorena Dunbar, Jamison Elder, and William Walters, that would be the case."

The diner was starting to fill up now. The music of plates and silverware clattering lent some extra percussion to the rock 'n' roll.

I asked, "Is it a condition of the will that Dex, Wake, and Dorena live at that mansion until their respective trust funds kick in?"

He seemed slightly surprised by that question. I had a feeling he didn't think I was capable of coming up with that one.

"Actually, Mr. Hammer… yes."

"Why would Dunbar insist on such a thing?"

He thought for a moment or perhaps was just gathering his words. "I believe it was part of making sure Charles had the support he needed. So that the boy… now a man, as you say… would not be cut off from his family. Not that any of the 'children' object to the arrangement—enough money was set aside to run the household for twenty years. Living at the Dunbar place is financially expedient for all concerned."

I nodded, getting that. "How limited are the funds Dorena, Dex, and Wake will be receiving till trust fund time?"

The droops on the eyes went up like window shades. "I'm not sure that telling you that, Mr. Hammer, is what Dorena had in mind when she asked me to talk with you."

I rolled out my nasty grin. "I heard her call you, Mr. Hines. I was standing right there. She told you to tell me whatever I wanted to know. And I want to know."

He sighed. His eyes drooped again in surrender. "Well, it's what each trust fund generates—about fifty thousand yearly for each of them. A handsome stipend, but for children who grew up wealthy, a bit of a challenge to live within those means."

I could use that kind of stipend myself.

Debbie brought more coffee for me, a fresh cup already with milk and sugar. She was growing on me.

"Now I do have to ask you something, counselor," I said, "that might go beyond what you feel comfortable sharing."

"At this stage, I can't imagine what that might be."

"Well, let's start with this. Wake Dunbar is my client, separately and in addition to what his sister has hired me to do. In both cases, I work through a Manhattan attorney with the proper paperwork. That grants me client confidentiality."

"An intelligent arrangement, sir."

"You don't have to sound surprised about it." I sipped the coffee. Perfect. "I assume, beyond being executor of the estate, that you do all the legal work for the Dunbars."

"That's correct."

"Can you confirm that if Wake and Madeline split up, she gets no share of the trust-fund money."

"I can."

My eyes narrowed in on him. "What if Wake should die before he reaches forty?"

"She gets it all."

"Full service, no waiting?"

He shrugged, gesturing with an open hand. "None. That was the prenup, which did, in fact, make its way into the will. Chester Dunbar knew all about it and approved heartily. Frankly, I don't think he ever cared for the woman."

"And why is that?"

"Well… I shouldn't share this because he told me in confidence."

"Why stop now, counselor?"

His mouth twitched under the fringe of mustache. "She was always… 'putting the make' on Chester, as I heard him say. By which I mean… inappropriate sexual advances."

"I know what 'putting the make on' means," I said. "What's her background, anyway?"

"She was a showgirl at a high-end nightclub. The Copa, I believe. That's where Wake saw her, and met her. Chester never approved." The attorney smirked humorlessly. "I suppose one can't blame the woman for trying to win her father-in-law's approval."

"Sure," I said, jamming on my hat. "But by screwing him?"

Hines was having a second piece of pie as I left. I noticed him pouring something from a flask into his coffee—not milk, I'd wager. Behind the counter, Debbie winked at me on my way out and I winked back. But in her case it might have been a twitch.

For a while I just sat outside the sleek diner in the Galaxie going over the legal niceties and not-so-niceties I'd just been made privy to. All I came up with was that everybody at the Dunbar place had a reason to want everybody else dead.

CHAPTER SIX

The neon glowed in the night, all in red: HONEST ABE'S LOG CABIN, with a tilted stovepipe hat shorting in and out. Nestled in a copse of pines a few miles outside of Monticello, the club itself lived up to its name, a log cabin, one-story with wings jutting at either side, the half-full gravel parking lot between. That's where I parked Dorena Dunbar's red Thunderbird—she'd let me drive—and came around and got the door for her, doing the gentleman bit.

When I'd got back to the Dunbar place late afternoon, I found that no one except Chickie and Dorena would be home for supper. Dixie the cook hadn't started anything yet, so I invited Dorena to accompany me for the evening. Chickie apparently was used to dining alone, in which event he got hot dogs, a favorite. Everybody won.

Here in the parking lot, under the full moon, Dorena was a lovely creature glowing in ivory. She wore a light-blue leather-belted sheath that showed off her slender shapely figure to a tee, topped off with a matching beret. I'd put on a fresh suit, if you're interested. The night was pleasantly cool, the thaw holding on.

I checked my hat—I hadn't worn the Burberry—and we passed by a bar with a Rat Pack feel and were quickly seated in a dining room where log-siding hugged booths that corralled thirty or so tables with chairs. The upper walls were smooth and decorated with muskets, Winchesters, and Indian artifacts.

Dorena had a Pink Lady, and mine was Four Roses and ginger. We sipped while we waited for our steaks to come. We chatted.

"Do you expect me," she said with a twinkle, "to believe you picked this place by chance?"

"Whatever do you mean," I said flatly. I don't twinkle.

She leaned forward, as if to keep this revelation from the several vacant tables beside our booth; the dining room was only lightly populated. "This Abe character is who my brother Dex is into, for a small fortune."

"Do tell."

"No, you tell. You can't suspect Abe What's-It of killing Jamison… or my father, for heaven's sake."

"That's right. I don't."

She eyed me with friendly suspicion. "You're here for my brother. What, to make his case for being good for the money?"

That was close enough. "Exactly," I said.

She sat back. "Well, that's fine by me. I think it's terrible the way some people prey on the weaknesses of others."

"If they didn't," I said with a shrug, "what would you have to write plays about?"

She gave me a chin-crinkling grin. "You're making fun of me, aren't you?"

"Not at all. Anyway, not very."

She leaned forward conspiratorially again. "Do you need extra money?"

"Who doesn't?"

"I mean... for doing this for Dex."

"No. He asked for a favor and I'm giving it to him. You've already been plenty generous."

When she had finished her queen filet and I'd put away my New York Strip, I ordered us another round of drinks. As we sipped those, I asked, "Will I be making anybody jealous tonight?"

"What do you mean?"

"Surely a lovely girl like you has a man in her life. Or men."

Dorena shook her head; the beret kept up with her. She looked like Bonnie Parker if a Hollywood star played her.

"Nobody," she said.

"Well, I count myself lucky I caught you between suitors." I kept that light, but she really was a beautiful thing. Also a client. And there was Velda to consider.

Did I mention she was a beautiful thing?

"I've had men in my life," she admitted. "But it never lasts."

"Why is that? Have they been out of their minds?"

She sipped her Pink Lady. "Maybe I'm hard to get along with."

"I can't see that. Are you afraid they're only after your money?"

"Good grief," she said, smiling, "I won't get my money for a lot of years."

But it *was* a lot of money.

"Anyway," she said, shrugging, "most of the guys I've dated were of the same… financial class."

That made sense. Minnows ran with minnows, sharks with sharks.

"Well," I said, "you being available is a mystery this detective can't solve."

She said nothing. She had that blankness a beautiful woman can get when she's thinking.

I said, "I'm prying. I'm sorry. It's my detective's nature."

A smile blossomed—a tiny one, as usual coral-tinged, but it did blossom. "Mike, with the last guy… I broke it off. I *always* break it off." A tiny shrug. "And I think the word has gotten around. I can't say the phone has been ringing off the hook."

"Do they get too fresh, these men you break it off with?"

She laughed. Damn near giggled. "No! I'm no virgin."

"Duly noted. Then why?"

Her sigh was deep and troubled. No giggling now. "Getting serious with anyone is out of the question. Getting married… it's just not for me."

I reached across and patted her hand. "Honey, you'd make some lucky slob a great wife. And some lucky kids a wonderful mother. Look at how you handle Chickie."

And she started to cry.

I came around on her side of the booth, slid in, and slipped an arm around her. She was dabbing her eyes with a clean corner of her napkin.

She swallowed. "Sorry… sorry."

"*I'm* sorry, doll. I caused this. What did I say?"

"It's just… Chickie… the way he is… the kind of child I might have…"

And I knew what it was that so terrified her: her brother's condition might be genetic, and she might carry that into a marriage, and motherhood. Pat had told me, and now so had she.

"Have you talked to the medics about it?"

She shook her head.

I shook mine. "Then these are just fears, not facts. I understand why you feel them, but you need to check this out and—"

"What Chickie has," she said, "isn't something the doctors know about."

"Well, sure it is, honey."

But she shook her head again, firmly, and I could tell there was no talking to her about it. I squeezed her shoulder, kissed her cheek, and got back across from her in the booth.

Then she excused herself and went off to fix her make-up. Light as she preferred it, that shouldn't take long. It didn't. She looked fresh and young again, getting in the booth across from me. I hated that she was suffering from what had to be a misconception about her situation.

"Now, it was not my intention," I said, "to spoil your evening. What say we go have a little fun? What's your pleasure? Roulette? Blackjack?"

"Oh, no," she said, eyes wide. "I'm too intimidated to *really* gamble. I'm afraid slots are my speed."

"Nothing wrong with that."

The casino took up a wing, and to get in, you had to be a member of the Log Cabin Club. It cost five whole bucks. Dorena was already a member. Inside, the cabin motif continued, bottom third of the walls log-siding, upper two-thirds smooth and all cowboys and Indians. Slots were lined up against every wall like St. Valentine's Day victims, and three roulette tables were going, business in here much better than in the dining room.

There were half a dozen blackjack stations, and toward the back some poker tables. Cute waitresses in short, fringed cowgirl skirts and Dale Evans hats were threading through, giving gamblers free drinks. I also noted half a dozen burly types in tuxedos who did not look like social directors.

I gave Dorena a twenty to get some quarters for the slots, and she protested, but I told her she could pay me back when she turned forty. She was just heading for the window to get herself some quarters when I spotted Dex, and I stopped her with a gentle hand on her arm.

"Who's that with your brother?"

I was referring to a brick-shithouse brunette with short, curly hair, wearing a paisley red-green-black sheath that hugged her the way most men would like to. Her face was heart-shaped, her nose pug, her lips lush and very red-lipsticked.

"That's Dex's latest," she said offhandedly. "Brenda Something."

That's how Wake had put it. Maybe her last name was Something.

I asked, "What do you know about her?"

"She works in a beauty shop. She'd like to be rich someday. What else do you need to know?"

"Doesn't she already have a husband?"

"Not a rich one. Anyway, they're separated, Dex says. But that doesn't stop the husband from getting jealous."

"Thanks," I said, and shooed her toward the nearest wall of slots.

I went over to where Dex could see me and nodded and smiled at him, and he nodded back. He was concentrating. Brenda Something, at his side, gave me one of those looks. You know the kind. The I-could-have-her-if-I-wanted variety. Why aren't all girls so friendly?

Here's the thing about Dex playing blackjack: he stunk.

He split tens, hit on hard fifteen when the dealer had a six up, and stood on an ace three. When he lost, he would double the size of his next bet, apparently thinking he'd only need to win once to get even. Sucker play.

No wonder he was in so deep to the house.

I was keeping an eye on the bouncer types. Two of them were talking, half a room away, nodding toward me. One nodded again and went off somewhere. I figured I'd been made. So much for no such thing as bad publicity.

Fifteen minutes disappeared, and so did fifteen-hundred of Dex's dollars. He was hunkered over with the miserable look of a guy who had been working an assembly line for way too long. Then Brenda whispered in his ear and she drifted off.

I followed her to the ladies' room and, not being a pervert, waited till she came back out before approaching her.

"How about a real drink?" I asked her.

"Pardon?" She gave me that toss of the head that tells a man that he's gone too far and hasn't gone far enough.

I gave her an openly lecherous grin. "You're better than these watered-down free drinks. You can only watch your boy friend lose for so long before it gets depressing."

She laughed a little and said, "I'll say," and took the elbow I offered.

We sat at the bar. I had another Four Roses and ginger and she ordered a Daiquiri.

"You're Brenda," I said, when we'd both finished our first drinks.

She was sitting sideways, facing me, her legs crossed. They were nice legs, dress hiked a little. She had red kitten heels on. Subtle she was not, but I liked her.

"How do you know my name?" she wondered.

"I asked somebody. Do you have a last name?"

"Sure. Everybody does."

"What is it?"

"Sundein."

Close to "Something," at that.

She asked, "Do you have a first name?"

"Mike. I have a last name, too."

She shrugged. "I don't really care. What do you think about a guy who takes a girl out and ignores her?"

I was doing that at the moment with Dorena. "He's a louse."

"Why do I stick with a guy like that?"

"Well, isn't he a Dunbar? Don't they have dough?"

She sighed. "They do. Not right now, maybe. But eventually."

"Didn't you used to have a ring on the fourth finger of your left hand?" I could see the white ghost of it. "A diamond maybe?"

She leered at me. "Why, did you find it?"

I leered at her. "Why, did you lose it?"

She laughed heartily at that; snorted a little. Possibly

not her first Daiquiri of the night.

"Did you *used* to have a husband?" I asked. "Or do you still have one?"

"In between."

"What does that mean?"

"We're separated. Not his idea, but... we're separated."

"That's too bad."

"No it isn't."

"Too bad for him, I mean. Losing out on a dish like you."

"You're a little fresh," she said, but she liked it.

I made my Four Roses and ginger last, but after her third Daiquiri, she proposed that we go outside and get a little fresh air. She had the keys to Dex's Lincoln and suggested we sit in back for a while and talk. That seemed like a fine idea to me.

Her kisses were hot and sticky and sloppy as hell, but not a bad time at all, and when I asked her, "Why did you break up with him?" (meaning her husband), she kissed me again, and her tongue went looking for my tonsils. Then she backed away a full three inches from my face and said, "He's unreasonably jealous."

That's as far as it went—some necking, some very heavy petting, but my fly and her dress stayed zipped. It was our first date, after all. I leaned against the Lincoln and lit up a Lucky. She was standing where the moonlight let her fix her make-up; she'd brought her purse along for the fun.

The guy came out of nowhere. He was tall enough

to be the original Honest Abe, and had the same kind of sinewy look as that legendary wrestling president. Narrow-faced, handsome in a Senior Boy Most Likely To Succeed sort of way, he was in a sportshirt and slacks and a rage.

He yanked her by the arm and almost hurled her to the gravel. "Is this him?" he snarled, pointing his finger at me. "Is *this* your rich boy friend?"

Her eyes were white all around. "Roger, stay away from me. I'll get a court order!"

He shoved her and she went down on her ass.

That was enough. I tossed the cig and grabbed him by the arm and swung him around, right into my right fist. Now *he* was on his ass. Brenda, sitting, leaning on her hands, started laughing.

I'd hit him hard, but he didn't care. He came up all at once, fists ready, charging like a bull. I kicked him in the stomach and he went down, retching. I was just about to kick his teeth in when I felt Brenda at my side, tugging on my arm, saying, "That's enough, Mike. That's enough."

And it was. She was beating the poor bastard up bad enough for the both of us. I walked her back inside, and she ducked into the bathroom again, then emerged to return to watching Dex lose.

I went into the men's john and splashed some water on my face; otherwise, I was none the worse for wear. Hadn't been much of a scuffle.

Dorena was winning. The tray below her slot

machine was swimming with quarters. She smiled at me. "What have you been up to?"

"The usual. Picking up women and making out with them."

"Oh, you. Are you ready to go?"

"No, keep playing. I need to try to see somebody."

I had already spotted the door with the sign that said OFFICE—PRIVATE. A burly bastard with shoulders so broad you had to look at them one at a time was standing by that door like a eunuch guarding the entrance to a harem. I didn't know they made tuxes that big.

I approached him with a smile, hoping he was muscle-bound enough to make handling him as easy as Brenda Something's spouse. Or Brenda for that matter.

"Mike Hammer," I said, figuring word was around that I was on the premises, "to see Mr. Hazard."

The guy had the sloping brow that goes with the job, and little flecks of white scar here and there. He had a blond crew cut, and you could smell the Butch Wax.

"You expected?" he asked, spitting the words like tobacco.

"No," I said, "but ask Abe if he'll see me."

He thought about that, as still as a statue and just as intelligent. Then he said, "You're *that* Mike Hammer?"

"How many are there?"

"Would you stand for a frisk?"

"No. But I'm unarmed." And I was.

"Then why wooden cha stand for a frisk?"

"Because I don't like men's hands on me."

He thought about that. That seemed reasonable.

"You stay here," he advised me pointlessly, and went in.

The eunuch wasn't gone long. He opened the door for me and gestured graciously. I went in alone.

Abe Hazard got up from behind a big old oaken desk as scarred as his bodyguard's face. Abe was short and fat but rather handsome, Robert Taylor's head on Stubby Kaye's body. He wore a beard like that of his namesake, a fun touch for the rubes.

He offered a plump hand for me to shake. What the hell. I shook it.

"It's been years, Mike," he said.

I knew of him but didn't remember ever meeting him. I said, "A long time."

"Also, we have mutual friends."

If he meant Carl Evello, who I tricked a stooge into killing, we did.

I said, "Small world."

He nodded to the chair opposite the desk. I took it. The office was nothing fancy, the same log-siding below and smooth cream walls above. A couch against one wall showed the wear of a body using it, and a couple of file cabinets huddled in one corner, as if waiting for a raid; on the walls were framed pictures of Abe and celebrities who'd stopped by the Log Cabin: Sinatra, Tony Bennett, Joe DiMaggio.

My host folded his hands on his uncluttered desk

MIKE HAMMER

as if about to say grace. "My staff *told* me we had a celebrity in the house."

His "staff" were those Neanderthal types in tuxes.

I gestured to the wall of frames. "Did you want to take my picture?"

He laughed. "No, Mike, I just wanted to say hello. And, uh, my people noticed you were watching my pal Dex Dunbar playing blackjack."

"I was. He's lousy. No wonder you consider him a pal."

His smile had a plastered-on look. "I saw in the *News* that you were the one who found that butler's body."

"I found half of it."

He offered me a cigar in a brass humidor. I shook my head. He selected one and got it going.

"So," my host said, "is that what brings you to the area? Dex and the other Dunbars?"

"Are we just making conversation, or is this business? I'm prepared to talk business, if you are."

Cigar smoke seeped through his smile. "All right, Mike. I'll bite. What is your business with me?"

"Dexter Dunbar is into you heavy. One hundred grand heavy—judging by the way I saw him playing tonight, probably more by now."

Abe shrugged a bulky shoulder.

I continued: "I understand you've been leaning on him to pay up. Yet you know he doesn't have the dough right now. So it's a dodge to get him to sign over a healthy chunk of his inheritance."

Abe's hands were still folded. He was twiddling his goddamn thumbs. "That *is* business, Mike… just not yours."

"Actually it is. Somebody took two shots at Dex a few days ago. He wants me to find out who might want him dead. I was thinking maybe nobody wanted him dead. Maybe somebody just wanted to spook him a little."

"And you think I might have done that?"

"Not you personally. Maybe one of your bully boys out there, if any of their thick clumsy paws can still hold a rod."

The plastered-on smile started to crack. "That's a very old-fashioned word, Mike—rod. You're like something out of another time."

"So is my .45. But it gets the job done."

He sighed. Shook his head a little. The handsome face on the circus fat-man body worked up a frown. "Threats. Tough talk. This is the sixties, Mike. That time is over. Don't be a relic."

"Said the guy in the log cabin. Look, I'm just here to say if anybody touches Dex Dunbar, they answer to me. Got that?"

The plump little hands came up, their palms facing me. "You need to think this through, Mike. In just a few years, Dex will have over a million dollars to play with. You saw him out there tonight—do I need any help getting him to give me money?"

"You've been threatening him."

"There's been some negotiation, yes. But my people didn't shoot at him. I want him alive and gambling. Where I'm headed in these negotiations is getting him to sign an agreement to pay me back with interest when his trust-fund money comes in."

"Loan shark interest?"

He shook his head. "No. Standard banker's interest."

"Would you be willing to show me that agreement, after you've negotiated it with Dex? Before he's signed it?"

"Yes. Why not?" He tamped cigar ash into a round glass Log Cabin tray. "Now. Is there anything else I can do for you? Arrange a line of credit with the house, perhaps?"

I stood. "No thanks. I'm not a gambler."

Abe chuckled. "How can you say that with a straight face, Mike?"

He had a point. And he was also right that his best play was to let Dex keep losing and racking up interest for the few years between him and his inheritance. Nothing wrong with getting the Dunbar loot on the instalment plan.

I nodded to Dex as I passed his blackjack table. He nodded back. Brenda gave me a smile, a rather sweet one, and a little-girl wave. I collected Dorena at her slot machine. She was seventy-five dollars and twenty-five cents ahead.

In the parking lot, she paused as I held the door open for her. She said, "I saw you go into that office."

"You did, huh?"

"Yes. You talked to that Abe person, didn't you?"

"I did."

"Did you straighten everything out for Dex?"

"More or less."

She showed me a nice coral smile. "Good," she said, and gave me a kiss. It wasn't hot and sloppy and sticky, but it wasn't bad.

When we got back to the Dunbar place, around eleven, I pulled Dorena's Thunderbird into its space in the garage. Dex's Lincoln was still gone, of course, and Wake's Jaguar was M.I.A. as well. But Madeline's little green Triumph TR4 was snug in its spot.

I climbed out of the T-bird and came around to open the door for Dorena. As I walked her up to the house, I said, "I thought Madeline was out for the evening."

"I did, too. She almost always is."

"I need to ask her a few questions."

"Oh?"

I nodded. "She was in the house the night your father died, and she'll eventually benefit from your butler's death."

That was all true, but really I was thinking about Wake and the broken stair-step in the garage and the brake-hose puncture in his Jag.

"If she's back," Dorena said, "I can tell you where to find her."

Off the kitchen was the TV room, an unpretentious

space that had once been a bedroom for live-in staff. A blond TV/stereo console was against the wall to my left as I entered, with shelving above perfect for the extensive LP collection. By the windowed sidewall, a card table was set up with four chairs and two waiting decks. On the cushioned window seat were casually stacked board games, Monopoly and Clue and the like, and a few jigsaw puzzles. Along the wall to my left was a zebra-striped bar with black-cushioned stools.

Facing the TV, in the middle of a three-seater brown leather couch on a braided rug, sat a beautiful redhead, her bare feet crossed on a matching ottoman. Her toenails were bright red. So was her lipstick, that mouth so swollen-looking she might have been recovering from a nasty slap. Her emerald capri pants were a little too short for those long, muscular legs, and under the light green fuzzy sweater, she might be smuggling cantaloupes across the border. *Ben Casey* was on, the pretty nurse on screen.

"We haven't really met, have we?" Madeline asked in a throaty purr that must have taken a while to perfect.

"No. But you know who I am."

"I do. You're Mike Hammer, who makes such a hit in the tabloids."

"A hit in the tabloids can be very painful."

She laughed at that and patted the seat next to her. "Join me."

I did. "I need to ask you a few questions."

She wiggled fingers at the TV. "Not till after my

show. Then it's the news and who gives a damn? We can talk during commercials, too."

Well, the show was almost over anyway. The plot was the guest star was sick and Dr. Ben Casey was treating it. Wake Dunbar's wife smelled of Arpège perfume, which Velda sometimes used.

During the last commercial, I asked, "Didn't you go out tonight?"

She nodded. "But just for dinner. We talked about a movie, but I had shows on."

"You and your husband?"

She laughed again and gave me a sideways are-you-kidding look. "No, it was this guy who is very nice and has a good job, but God he's dull. If you were out with me, wouldn't *you* make a move?"

Only if I still had a pulse.

"Of course not," I said. "You're a married woman."

This time the sideways look had a smirk in it. "Are you really a detective?"

"Doesn't it show?"

She glanced at my lap. "Something does. Shush, shush… it's back on."

The patient lived, but Ben Casey didn't seem very happy about it.

She got up and leaned over as she turned off the TV, her rounded backside to me, and I was proud of myself for not passing out. She scooted back and curled up under those endless legs and stretched her arm along the top cushion behind me.

"Fire away," she said. She was smiling, eager to help. To please. Her make-up was a little overdone, mostly to hide freckles that would only have made her more genuinely beautiful.

"What can you tell me about the night your father-in-law died?"

She hadn't heard or seen anything. Her room was toward the other end of the hall. Her room? Or her and her husband's room? Another are-you-kidding look. She slept alone. When she was home.

What could she tell me about the butler? Not much. He was sweet, quiet, and really looked after Chickie well. Showed real affection for the boy, which is more than could be said for his stepbrothers.

"The unusual way Chester Dunbar's will is set up," I said, "everyone in the family, including yourself, would benefit from Elder's death. A quarter of a million is a lot of money."

"Split five ways? Chickenfeed, compared to a mil, right?"

"I suppose so. Isn't a million what you'd inherit if Wake died?"

She batted that away, the red nails blurring past me. "He's healthy as a horse, my loving husband. No, Mike, I gotta wait this one out. Just a few more years."

"But I hear Wake is talking divorce now."

She shook her head, all that hair bouncing; she wore lime-green plastic earrings. "Not going to happen. He's not going to embarrass himself. It's all a bluff."

"Embarrass himself? Why?"

Her expression flickered; perhaps she'd spoken too freely. She said, "Well, not because I'm a little round-heeled whore, as he so affectionately likes to call me. Not *that*."

And I had it. Separate bedrooms. Trips nightly into the Village. Those delicate features, the artistic bent. *Wake was gay*. Madeline was his live-in beard. Only she wasn't behaving. But could he risk outing himself in a divorce case?

"I understand," I said carefully, "that Wake's had a few narrow scrapes of late."

She shrugged. "Not that he's told me about. Of course, we don't exactly communicate much."

I told her about the broken step and the hole in the brake hose.

She was frowning now. "And Wake's implying *I'm* responsible?"

"Not necessarily," I lied.

"You ever consider he might be trying to make me look bad?"

"It did occur to me. Could I offer some friendly advice? It's free and worth every penny."

She nodded and all that lush red hair came along.

I said, "Try to work out a settlement with Wake. He's got fifty grand a year coming in and he's selling his paintings both here and in the Village. Come to an agreement for a monthly sum. Come to an agreement of what your share of the trust-fund money will be.

Then legally separate so that you-out-having-fun doesn't embarrass him or make you look bad."

This was the second time tonight a beautiful woman had looked at me with the blankness that conceals thought.

Then she said, "You're a nice man, Mike. A caring human being."

"I get that a lot."

She rose and went to the door and clicked the knob lock. The room was already dimly lit. She positioned herself between me and the TV and provided substitute entertainment, pulling the fuzzy sweater off and revealing twin braless globes of flesh with tiny hard tips. The sweater she tossed off with casual abandon. The capri pants came off with a little more effort, requiring a kind of shimmy. The only thing she had on were the lime-green earrings. She stepped out of the little capri pile and put her head back and her hands on her hips, legs apart, the thatch so red it burned.

"Would *you* rather hump a man?" she asked.

"No," I said.

She came over and sat sideways in my lap and nuzzled my neck. I gave her a kiss, to show I appreciated the effort, but then I held her face in my hands and said, "A lovely girl like you has nothing to prove."

Tears glittering like gems, she nodded.

I kissed her again, then made a hasty exit.

Damn! This lousy case came complete with hot and

cold running dames. I went up to my bedroom and climbed in the rack and tried not to think about what I'd just walked away from.

CHAPTER SEVEN

The drive to the Condon Hale estate on Long Island from Monticello took a good two-and-a-half hours. Near Glen Cove, in an area known for parking couples, trapshooters, and notorious recluses, I was here to see one of the latter. I turned at a sign that said PRIVATE PROPERTY—TRESPASSERS WILL BE SHOT.

What the hell, I was armed... but I was also expected. As if it had been dropped by a twister, an Edwardian mansion perched itself on a sandy, grassy bluff overlooking the beach. The place must have been built around the turn of the century, brown brick with fancy white wood trim, including a pillared front porch. But the old girl wasn't aging well—the brick could use re-grouting, the paint was blistering, the roof tiles loose, and instead of ladies and gentlemen in their Gibson girl dresses and high-hats formal attire, what you pictured was their tormented ghosts.

I left the Galaxie on the apron of the circular brick drive and went up a short flight to the porch, where I rang the bell.

A chauffeur answered. Not a butler—not in that gray livery, minus cap but including SS leather boots and pistol in a leather quick-snap holster. The sign did say trespassers would be shot, after all.

He opened the door maybe a third. He was a big man, bigger than me, with the hard-eyed, seen-it-all gaze of a combat veteran. He looked a little like Kirk Douglas without the chin dimple.

"Mr. Hammer?" His voice was a low rumble, like a car engine starting up. Well, he was the chauffeur, wasn't he?

"Yes," I said, removing my hat. "Michael Hammer."

He nodded. "I'm who you talked to on the phone. Mr. Hale is expecting you. He's waiting for you on the veranda. He enjoys the ocean."

"Who doesn't?"

The inside was in better shape than the out. The chauffeur moved me through a generous central hall where turn-of-the-century details blurred by—stained glass windows, dark sculpted woodwork, fancy light fixtures, all of the era. There was still a sense of gloom, though, and the antique furniture had seen use since before it was antique. But if I'd been expecting Miss Havisham's ruined mansion, I was mistaken.

I fell in beside him and asked, "How big a staff

does it take to maintain this place?"

We were moving past a slightly sunken low-ceilinged dining room with wide flat woodwork and small high windows. Dark in there. They used to think it helped the digestion.

"Only two of us are live-in," he said. "Mr. Hale's nurse and myself. But a cleaning crew comes in once a week. The upstairs has been closed off for some time, however."

So that was where I might expect to run into Miss Havisham and maybe get a slice of ancient wedding cake.

Finally we were in a big white kitchen that looked modern, or more modern than the rest of the place. Probably remodeled in the '30s. I asked, "What branch?"

He gave me a sideways look. "Army. Rangers."

"Not every day you meet a real live commando. Me, I was just another G.I. Joe."

"Where did you serve?"

"Pacific. You?"

"France. North Africa."

"You took the scenic route."

The veranda was fieldstone and provided a fine view of the ocean: foamy tide caressing the beach, gulls wheeling on a gray sky where the clouds were sparse, like dying smoke. A little too cold for swimmers, but this was likely private beach anyway.

The man in the wheelchair was small and shrunken, one of those skeletons you see in a doctor's office but with skin pulled over it, loosely. The scant hair on his head was like white wispy thread, the eyebrows a memory. He was ninety if a day, bundled in a red-and-black plaid blanket beneath which were heavy, dark flannel pajamas. What was left of his feet lived in fur-lined bedroom slippers, propped on the wheelchair footplate.

A wooden folding chair was set up next to him. The chauffeur gestured for me to sit, and I did, and he took a few paces back but stayed with us.

The old man hadn't looked at me or acknowledged me in any way, but he said, "Do you like the scent of the sea, Mr. Hammer?"

It appeared there would be no introductions.

"I do, Mr. Hale."

"How would you describe it?"

"Crisp, with a hint of algae. Salty. Bitter yet clean, fresh. Sometimes fishy but not today."

"You like the water."

"I do. I spend time in Florida now and then."

"I can't smell it at all."

"Oh?"

"Lost my sense of smell in a laboratory explosion some years ago. But do you believe me when I say I can *remember* how it smells? That I can feel on my face the *way* it smells, the breeze, the bite?"

"I do."

Now he looked at me, his eyes brown and bright in their sunken holes. "You want me to tell you about Jamison Elder and Chester Dunbar and me."

"I'd like that, yes."

"You think they were murdered—that all the talk of accidental death is bunk."

Gulls swooped, squawked, chirped, wailed, answering distant caws.

"They were murdered, all right."

"You know this, Mr. Hammer?"

"Call it an educated guess. I know something about murder."

His nod almost creaked. "Yes, I've heard of you. Read of you. You are an energetic young man."

Not so young, but compared to this coot, a baby. Still, something remained very much alive in that bloodless, skin-draped skull.

"Tell me what you know about murder, Mr. Hammer."

"That would take all day, Mr. Hale."

"I have time."

Actually, he didn't have all that much time, did he?

I said, "My time is limited, Mr. Hale. I have a meeting with a NYPD Homicide captain this afternoon."

His laugh was like someone had hit him in the stomach. "Murder again. Tell me at least a *few* things about murder, Mr. Hammer. From your experienced vantage point."

I shrugged. "Well, it doesn't just happen. It's planned. Sometimes in haste, but it's planned or else it's just manslaughter."

"So we're talking legal definitions, then?"

"That figures in. The other thing about murder is

that, nine times out of ten, there's cold hard cash at the root of it."

"Root of all evil, they say."

"There's a book that's written in, yeah. But the list of motives is surprisingly short—love, greed, revenge, and lunacy. Everything else is a variation on those themes."

The gulls were making lazy circles now.

"Or a combination thereof, Mr. Hammer?"

"Or a combo, yeah."

"Do you suspect me of murder, Mr. Hammer?"

"I don't know enough about the trouble between you and Jamison Elder, and Chester Dunbar for that matter, to make that judgment. I doubt sincerely that a man in your physical state could have murdered anybody, even three years back. But that commando chauffeur of yours sure could. And with his skills, he could get in and out of a house without a soul any the wiser."

I didn't glance back at the guy, but I could hear his breathing go deep.

Condon Hale laughed; it sounded like paper rustling. "My man Reeves would be capable of that and much more, Mr. Hammer. You are correct. He could dispose of you this afternoon, and who would know?"

"He could try."

"*Reeves!* Show Mr. Hammer out."

The chauffeur came at me quick, but I was out of the chair fast enough to swing it at him; it broke like kindling. He was all muscle, even twenty years after the war. And I was only in fair shape—not long ago I had made a seven-year habit of getting the shit kicked out of me and waking up all puffy in a gutter.

His fists were extended, stretching out for me, but all the muscles in the world won't save you when a hard heel slams into your knee. He went down on the other one, smacking the fieldstone, his face clenching, but his eyes were open enough to see the .45 staring him in the face.

I reached down and unsnapped the holster and tossed his gun way down on the sand.

"Go in the house," I told him, with a friendly wave of the weapon, "and stay there. I don't mean any offense—we're just a couple of slobs doing their jobs. But if I see you come back out, I'll assume you're armed and I'll kill your ass."

He knew I wasn't kidding. He wasn't even mad about it, at least not that it showed. This guy was a pro, which I liked, but I would stay nice and alert as long as I was on the Condon Hale grounds.

"Impressive," the old man said, his smile like a fold in parchment. "Reeves isn't easily handled. He was in the Rangers, you know."

I had no chair to sit on now. So I just loomed over him. "And I killed enough Japs to stack up to your chimney, and can we stop playing goddamn games, Mr. Hale?" I put the .45 back in the shoulder sling. "Nobody's threatening you. Nobody's accusing you of anything. But I came into the picture late. I even missed the cartoon. So fill me in."

He looked toward the sea. A gull dive-bombed, after a fish.

"I allowed you to come today, Mr. Hammer, because I wanted you to know where I stand."

"You don't stand at all. You're in a fucking wheelchair. And if you think I wouldn't roll you into that surf and dump you, you haven't been paying attention."

The bright eyes in the sunken holes turned slowly to me, a ship changing course. "You must understand one thing, Mr. Hammer, and understand it completely. I have no desire to help the Dunbar family. My family, my children, are all grown and on their own, and productive, responsible members of society. These Dunbar brats are the kind of sad, selfish lot that Chester Dunbar so richly deserved. And now *you* are working for them."

So that was the roadblock.

"My client," I said, "is the NYPD Homicide man I mentioned earlier. Chester Dunbar was his first precinct captain. Dunbar may have been a thieving rat by the time you knew him, but back in those days, he was just a cop. Apparently a damn good one. Would you begrudge my cop friend from trying to see if his old captain was murdered?"

He was looking at the ocean again. The gun-metal gray waves were getting a little angry, the lap of the tide edging up the beach.

"I would imagine," the old man said, "that you know I am... or at least was... an inventor myself. I have several major patents, going back well before the war."

I nodded.

"After the war, I came up with a cardiac pulse-rate monitor, which alerts its wearer of an irregular heartbeat by using an electric-powered magnet. I began to explore related possibilities."

"Was Chester Dunbar part of that?"

"Not initially. But he'd had some success with a radar device that he essentially gave to the government for the duration. Post-war, he was starting to earn royalties, but he was all too eager to go into partnership with me, and the financial backing that represented."

The lap-lap-lap of the ocean was providing a hypnotic soundtrack beneath the old man's droning, oddly distant words.

He went on: "We were working together on a prototype for a heart rhythm recording device. Things were going well. Suddenly Chester quit, claiming there were demands on his time due to the radar device, which was really starting to earn significant dollars. But I later learned that, while working in my lab, Chester was readjusting my prototype when a familiar rhythm resounded: the human heart's two-pulse beat. He knew at once what that meant. And from this accident came the pacemaker, which he patented himself."

"And he didn't cut you in?"

"No. He denied the work he'd done in my lab, on my dime, had anything to do with his discovery. What he *did* do was hire away my longtime 'loyal' chauffeur,

Jamison Elder, who was a witness to the circumstances of the discovery. He paid Elder handsomely, I understand. And while I won a limited share of the profits—in a protracted, expensive court battle—the lion's share, and the credit, went to Dunbar, in part because of Elder's testimony."

"Getting back to murder motives," I said, "you have two—greed *and* revenge."

His smile was thin and rumpled but wide. "You look at a man content, Mr. Hammer. Content in knowing that the bastards who stole from him are dead and gone. That they may have died under mysterious, possibly violent circumstances, just adds to my satisfaction." The sunken eyes swung sharply toward me. "But I had nothing to do with it. Either death! You've heard of karma?"

"I've heard of kismet."

"Both apply. Now, if you'd like to make your way to your vehicle—without going through the house and perhaps having another, possibly less successful encounter with Reeves—you might cut around between the main building and the guesthouse to get to the drive. Unless you have further questions, Mr. Hammer?"

I didn't.

He was staring at the ocean, its surface as gray as his, gulls cawing, waves rolling, when I headed around the house. Why mess with a commando if you don't have to?

* * *

She was crowding fifty and a pleasant-looking woman made haggard by the situation. Her blue-and-brown plaid cotton dress was simple but crisp and fairly new. Her short, permed hair was dishwater blonde and her face had angles and pock-marked cheeks, but the eyes were big and dark blue and lovely. She was in a chair next to the desk in Captain Pat Chambers' modest office, facing me where I sat in the visitor's chair. My hat was on Pat's desk and I was sitting forward.

The introductions had already been made—this was Mrs. Lucille Carter of Middletown, Delaware, a fifth-grade school teacher who had taken a day off without pay to come to New York City and identify her brother's grisly remains.

She had already accomplished that unpleasant task, but Pat had asked her to meet with me before heading back home.

Mrs. Carter was shaking her head. "Mr. Hammer, I have no idea why my brother told various people that I was ill, and that he needed to rush home to my side. I wasn't at all sick, and even if I had been, frankly, my brother and I were not terribly close."

"Were you estranged?" I asked.

"Oh, heavens no. He was just much older than I, and we only saw each other at Christmas and other family get-togethers. I have another brother and two sisters, and Jamie was the oldest."

Pat had heard all of this already, but he was paying rapt attention anyway. His tie was loose and he was in his shirtsleeves. It was sixty degrees in the city. Odd to think the discovery of that ice floe and its half a passenger had only been a few days before.

I asked, "What can you tell us about your brother? What sort of man was he?"

She shrugged. "Quiet. Quite intelligent. I always thought that working as a domestic, however well he was paid, was beneath his abilities. I know he and Mr. Dunbar were very tight, almost best friends, or as much so as a servant can be with a master."

That was a kind of quaint way to put it, but I knew what she meant.

"Mrs. Carter," I said, "what did your brother have to say about working at the Dunbar place?"

She opened a hand. "He claimed to enjoy it. To find it rewarding. But to me his life was wasted there. He spent so much of his time at that place, and never really had the kind of, well, rich, rewarding social life a person needs."

"You mean, he never married?"

"Well… that's part of it. He went out with a few women over the years, and once or twice it seemed serious. But he was so blessedly devoted to the Dunbars, particularly that boy, that he was never able to make the leap."

"That boy—Chickie?"

"That's right. Charles." She shook her head. "There's something wrong with that boy, and there's something *very* wrong, even… despicable… about the father never getting his son help. Judging by what Jamie said, I would think the child is autistic. But apparently no doctors… or at least very few… have ever examined him."

Pat, eyes narrowed, said, "That does seem odd. Did your brother ever speak to that?"

"Only in a dismissive way. He seemed convinced that he was doing everything for that boy that could be done."

"That boy," I said, "is twenty now."

"In literal years, perhaps. Developmentally, more like ten." She paused. "That's wrong of me to say. I never met the boy, the young man… everything I got was secondhand, from Jamie. And Jamie was very concerned, very protective of him. He home-schooled Charles, you know."

I nodded. "When did you last have contact with your brother?"

"Oh, I guess… the Christmas before last. Not even a phone call from him to me, or me to him, since. Not a letter from either of us. Isn't that awful? Isn't that terrible?"

She began to cry, quietly, her head bowed a little. Pat had placed a box of tissues near her and she reached for one. We waited.

"Such… such a waste of a promising life," she said. "Jamie was the smartest of us all—valedictorian of his class. But the family couldn't afford college, and somehow he wound up with that terrible inventor out on Long Island."

"Condon Hale," I said. "I interviewed him this morning."

She made a face. "That creature accused Jamie of theft, and later, perjury. There was a big, embarrassing court case, you see. That's what created the bond between him and Chester Dunbar, I believe—they had both been attacked by the same scurrilous individual."

I nodded. "How bad was the blood between Hale and your brother, and your brother's employer?"

Another shrug. "It all quieted down after Hale got his settlement."

But the old man had still seemed plenty bitter today, despite the passage of years.

She leaned forward and her eyes met mine and held them. "Mr. Hammer, Captain Chambers has explained to me that you believe my brother may have been murdered. And also that the State Police aren't pursuing Jamie's death as such."

"You're right in both cases."

I told her, and Pat, about visiting the site of the supposed accident, and shared my own theory about what may have happened there.

"But Jamie had no enemies," she said, her expression bewildered.

I smiled just a little. "Meaning no disrespect, Mrs. Carter, you said yourself that you and your brother weren't close. There may have been many things going on in his life that you weren't aware of."

Her mouth tightened and then edged open as she

somewhat defensively said, "I knew my brother. I knew his character. What kind of man he was."

"I'm sure you did," I said. "But let's get back to Jamie borrowing a car and telling everyone at the Dunbar estate that he was rushing home to be at the side of your sick bed."

The defensiveness dropped away. She frowned more in confusion than anything else, and said, "That's what mystifies me so. I have no explanation for that."

"Well, obviously it indicates he was hiding something from the Dunbars."

"I don't know much about them," she admitted. "From what little I heard of them from Jamie, he thought highly of the daughter... what is her name?"

"Dorena."

She nodded. "He thought highly of Dorena, and just sort of... put up with those two brothers. They're stepchildren, I understand. He got along well with that caretaker, Walters, who he said was a real help with young Charles."

Pat turned to me. "Anything else, Mike?"

I shook my head, then smiled at Jamison Elder's sister. "Thank you, Mrs. Carter, for taking time to talk to me."

Her smile was as warm as it was sad. "No, Mr. Hammer—thank *you*. Captain Chambers has explained that he has no jurisdiction in Jamie's death, and that the State Police appear to have written it off as accidental. Knowing that an experienced investigator like yourself is looking into things is most reassuring."

"Glad to do it."

"In fact, I wonder if I might help support your efforts." She got in her purse and fished out her checkbook. "Perhaps you could take me on as a client."

One thing I didn't need in this case was another client.

"No," I said, smiling, holding up two palms in "stop" fashion. "You're very kind, Mrs. Carter, but that end of things is covered."

"You... you found my brother, didn't you?"

I nodded, thinking, *What was left of him.*

"What was left of him," she said, and shivered. She shook her head and said, "Seeing him there on that slab... just the upper part of him... it was so horrific. So terrible."

I'd seen him on a slab, too.

She was saying, "Right there in the morgue, I told him something I never had before, I'm ashamed to say."

Pat asked, "What's that, Mrs. Carter?"

"That I loved him."

She used one last tissue, then forced a smile, got to her feet.

"Well," she said, "I have a train to catch. Back to Middletown to see what's left of my classroom after the little darlings no doubt subjected my substitute to a day of merry hell."

I was on my feet. Pat too. We both shook hands with her and thanked her again, then she slipped out. I sat back down and so did Pat.

"Not a lot of help," he said.

"Some."

"Such as what?"

"Her brother's devotion to Chester Dunbar and Chickie means something. I'm not sure exactly what yet, but it does. The man's whole life was at that Dunbar mansion, and yet the night he died he was fleeing there, under false circumstances."

Pat frowned in thought. "Are you maybe reading too much in?"

"You tell me, Pat. My guess is that one of the siblings is trying to weed out the competition for when Chet Dunbar's money starts getting split up between them."

"You have any evidence of that, Mike?"

Here's where the ice got very thin. Pat was my client—maybe only a buck's worth, but my client nonetheless. Then there was Dorena and her stepbrothers who hired me to look into the accidental deaths of Daddy and his butler. Fine so far—Pat's wishes tallied perfectly with theirs. But the two brothers who each thought somebody was trying to kill them, that got into areas of confidentiality and conflict of interest.

What the hell—I told him. Told him about the broken step and the damaged brake hose that made Wake suspicious of his wife, and told him about the two shots somebody took at Dex, who suspected casino boss Abe Hazard.

"Trouble is," I said, "Wake has as much reason to want his dearly beloved dead as she does him, so he could be trying to frame her for attempted murder."

Pat nodded. "And Abe Hazard tells a convincing story of why killing Dex makes no financial sense. But what about that hothead husband of Dex's latest squeeze—Brenda, was it?"

I smirked and pawed the air. "How could that dope have shot at Dex last week, when he mistook me for him last night? No, something else is going on."

"What about Condon Hale? Could his old grudge have turned into new murders?"

"Not committed by him. He's frail and in a wheelchair. But that ex-Ranger chauffeur of his could easily have done his bidding."

Pat looked glum. "Well, I tried to rattle Jim Sheridan's cage, but he's still on the fence. He admits you raise some interesting points, but he's not going to risk his next promotion by going to the B.C.I. and getting the horse laugh."

"These damn troopers think crime stops and starts with a speeding ticket."

He shrugged. "Jim's all right. You come up with something, he'll get right on it." His gray-blue eyes fixed on me. "What say you, Mike? You think you're getting close?"

"Not sure." I got up, stretched, yawned, and picked my hat off his desk. "But I'm gonna stay on it. You haven't got your buck's worth yet."

* * *

Velda was on the phone when I came in. I hung up
my coat but left my hat on, went over and took the
visitor's chair, rocking back in it as I waited, giving her a
cocky look. She was dealing with one of the insurance
companies we do regular work for. She was charming
as hell with the guy on the other end of the line, but
she stuck her tongue out at me.

I grinned and rocked some more.

"What brings you home, my wandering boy?" she
asked, after hanging up. She rose and went over to put
a folder in a file cabinet.

"You look great," I said.

And she did. What she could do with a cream-color
silk blouse, a short tan skirt and no nylons could curl
a censor's hair.

She came over and sat on the edge of the desk, legs
crossed as if to taunt me—strike the "as if."

"Don't think compliments are getting you out of
the doghouse," she said.

"What put me in?"

"Two days and not a phone call. You expect me to
stave off the clients looking to talk to you? I won't *do*,
you know. I'm not the famous Mike Hammer."

"What is it really, kitten?"

She looked down her pretty nose at me. "Pat says
you're staying at the Dunbar place. I've seen that
Dorena's picture on the society page. Whose bedroom
are you sleeping in?"

"Well, not her gay brother's. Look, it's a job. And a favor to Pat, who repays me by as soon as I'm out of the city starting to sow seeds of discontent to try to win you over."

"What seeds are *you* sowing?"

"You want to hear what I've been up to or not?"

She did. I filled her in. I edited a few things out, like how friendly Dorena had got and that Brenda Something had a way with a sticky kiss. I did mention that Madeline Dunbar was a bit of a wild one.

"How wild?" Eyebrows arched even as the dark eyes narrowed. "Do you speak from personal experience?"

I shrugged. "She got a little frisky."

Her arms were folded over the impressive shelf of her bosom. "Frisky, huh? I hope you didn't throw her a bone."

I put a hand on her knee. She didn't flick it off, which was a very good sign.

"Listen," she said. "You're getting popular. You got another of those cryptic unsigned letters."

She plucked an envelope, already opened, from a stack on the desk.

I removed the single sheet from within. "Don't you know it's a federal crime to open other people's mail?"

"I thought I'd risk it." She took back the envelope and waved it. "Monticello postmark again. Same high-quality paper. No return address, of course."

I read aloud from the typed copy: "'Necessity, Plato says, is the father of invention.' My fan is a show-off."

"He's also wrong. It's *mother* of invention, and Plato said something like that, but not exactly."

"Same precise use of commas," I commented.

"What's the message, Mike? Neither note was threatening."

"They're not threats, my darling girl. They're dares." I threw the sheet back on the desk, and my eyes met hers. "This case is heating up."

"Seems like it."

"I think it's time you came in off the bench."

Her whole manner changed. She didn't smile yet she blossomed somehow. "You have something for me?"

I reached in my pocket for a want ad I'd torn out of the *Sullivan County Democrat*. Handed it to her.

"Seems they need dolls to deliver drinks to gamblers," I said, "at Honest Abe's Log Cabin. Interested?"

CHAPTER EIGHT

When I got back to the Dunbar place, it was around eight, and the cook, Dixie, was already off for the day. I scrounged in the fridge, found some slices of corned beef and Swiss cheese, and helped myself to rye bread and hot mustard and a bottle of Blue Ribbon. I put together a sandwich fit for a top-notch deli, and a canister on the counter provided a bag of potato chips that made it a regular feast.

The kitchen had a Formica-topped table off to one side, not far from the rec room where not so long ago Madeline Dunbar had taken off her light-green fuzzy sweater for me. The door was closed but the muffled rumble of the TV was going. She might be in there right now, and who knew if this time I could maintain my virtue? So I just sat at the little table and chowed down. I was finished with the food but having a second

Blue Ribbon when the back door in the kitchen opened and Willie Walters shuffled in.

The scrawny caretaker with the wrinkled puss was once again in the white-and-black-and-red plaid hunter's jacket, but it was unzipped and the flap-ear hat was missing, revealing an unkempt thatch of gray hair. It was only around fifty-five degrees out there now.

Seeing me, he lit up like somebody threw a light switch. He hustled over and stood next to me, awkwardly.

"You don't suppose they's another one of them Pabst Blue Ribbons in that icebox?"

"Is that a rhetorical question, Willie?"

"What kind of what?"

I grinned and jerked a thumb over my shoulder. "Go ahead, Willie. I'll cover for you."

He got the beer and came over and sat next to me. He guzzled some suds, then said, "I saw you pull in."

"Right. You opened the gate for me."

"I mean, I been wanting to talk to you, and saw you was back from the city."

"Word gets around."

"A place like this it sure does. I heard today you went down to see Jamie's sister at Centre Street."

"I did," I said, with a nod between gulps of brew.

"How's she holdin' up?"

I shrugged. "She's doing all right, considering earlier she saw half of her brother on a morgue tray."

He shook his head, guzzled some more beer. "It's a shame. She's a nice gal. She really is."

"Why, Willie, did she come around here to visit Elder quite a bit?"

"No, no! But he always spoke highly of her. She's a school teacher, ain't she?"

"She is. But so in a way was her brother."

Humorless smirk and a nod. "Yep. He taught Chickie good. Really done well with the kid, all things considered."

"Chickie's not really a kid, any more. He's twenty, isn't he?"

Walters sighed. "Well, all kinds of ways, he's still pretty much a kid."

"I can tell you one thing, Willie. That young man is no idiot. He may be stunted in how he's developed, but there are brains in that noggin somewhere."

The caretaker finished off the beer, and let out a resounding burp. You don't want to know what it smelled like.

"Mr. Hammer, I been tryin' to fill in for Jamie, but these Dunbars need to find somebody else to help out with that boy. I ain't fit for doin' his schoolin'. I'll tell you one thing, though."

"Yeah?"

"He's really took a shine to you, yessir. When you was away today, he got real down at the mouth, real damn blue. You know, he's over in the carriage house. Watchin' *The Man from U.N.C.L.E.* long about now. You wouldn't wanna give the boy a boost, and go over and watch with him? I'd do it myself but the Dunbars want me to stay down in that guardhouse. You know, I had to shoo reporters away twice the other morning."

I drained the beer and said, "Sure. I'll go keep Chickie company a while. Kind of wanted to chat with him about things, anyway."

So I cleaned up after myself, then went out with Walters still at my side, chattering about this and that. We trotted over to the fieldstone path, which could only be directly accessed through the library, and made our way along. The two-story gray-stone carriage was silhouetted in the moonlight, and what had been snow-covered ground was now a patchwork of white and brown. The caretaker grinned as he pointed to the tilled ground at the rear of the building.

"Way this thaw is settin' in, we'll be working in that garden 'fore you know it. That's where I had Jamie all beat with that boy—gardening is *my* specialty."

Presumably not something he picked up as a guard in the Tombs.

When we got to the side door that opened onto the recreation room, Walters paused and said, "I best get back to my post. They's a fridge in there, but it's only got milk and pop in it. So if you want more beer, you'll have to hoof it back to the house."

Then he sauntered off, starting down the gentle slope.

I opened the door and it hit me: *the gas smell.*

That sulfurous, rotten-egg smell.

Chickie was settled deep in his comfy chair opposite the television, where Napoleon Solo and his Russian partner were bantering. The young man was in western-styled pajamas with the Lone Ranger on a breast pocket and on his matching slippers as well. His head was to one side and he was out.

Maybe dead.

I ran to him, gathered him in my arms like he really was a slumbering child and not a young man of twenty, and hustled him out into the crisp air, away from the mouth of that gas chamber.

Walters was well down the slope but still in sight and I yelled, "*Willie!* Get your ass up here! *Now!*"

He turned, startled, but paused for only an instant as he could see me in the nearly full moon's light with the human bundle sagging in my arms. By the time the caretaker reached me, I had rested my charge gently on the ground, finding a spot with neither snow nor mud, and I checked him over.

"He's breathing," I said.

"Jeez Louise! What *happened*, Mr. Hammer?"

"Gas leak maybe. I'm going back to take a look. Are you a smoker, Willie?"

"Sure. Why, you want a ciggie?"

"No, and right now neither do you. A spark would send that carriage house up like a Titan missile. Here— I'll help you get him to his feet. You strong enough to walk him by yourself, Willie?"

"I'll *make* myself that strong, Mr. Hammer."

The caretaker had Chickie on his feet now and was hobbling around with him. But he was mostly dragging the boy, who was not walking yet, not near conscious.

I took a deep breath of good, clean non-city air and went back into the place, fast. The first most logical culprit would be that gas fireplace in one corner, a black metal conical freestanding job. No fire was going, but the switch in back was at full throttle. I shut it off, then started throwing open windows. I leaned my head out the last one, grabbed some fresh air, and headed upstairs. The gas had found its way into the two bedrooms, though not so heavily as below, and I opened the windows up there as well.

When I emerged from the carriage house, I bent over with my hands on my knees and helped myself to some more untainted air. Walters was walking the boy now, Chickie conscious but stumbling.

I went over and got on the other side of the staggering young man, gripped him around the shoulders, and the caretaker and I drunk-walked him till he was fully conscious and able to stand without falling. Still holding onto him, we walked him up to the house and into the kitchen. I put him at the Formica-topped table and got him a glass of water from the tap.

He drank about a third of it, then sat there in his pajamas with his hands folded in say-grace fashion. I plopped down next to him, and he looked at me with his boyish face needing a shave.

"Mike, I fell asleep."

"You did at that."

"My tummy aches. My head hurts."

I put a hand on his shoulder and squeezed. "You'll get over that. Shouldn't take too long. There was a gas leak over at the carriage house."

"What's that?"

"Gas that heats a house or a stove can make you sick if it isn't handled right. Your room and that whole place has to be aired out. All the windows are open to let fresh air in. Follow, son?"

Maybe he did, because he nodded.

Walters, standing nearby, his concern making vertical lines of the wrinkles in his face, said, "You best not sleep over there tonight, Chickie."

I nodded. "We'll talk to Dorena and get you a bed here at the house."

As if I'd summoned her, Dorena came in from the TV room. Apparently she was the one watching in there tonight—no sign of Madeline. Her hair ponytailed back, Dorena was all in light blue—a blouse with an Italian collar and capri pants, her feet bare.

"What's going on out here?" she asked, not irritated, just confused, the big brown eyes bigger yet. I could hear the TV going. Sounded like *Peyton Place*.

I explained to her there'd been a gas leak, and watched her carefully to see how she reacted, since it wasn't a leak at all. Someone had thrown that lever to fill the carriage house with gas. She had no reaction except concern for Chickie, who she hugged; he hugged her back. She was either innocent of the crime, or very, very good.

Because it was becoming obvious that one of the siblings was trying to kill the others, to inherit the entire family fortune. And Dorena alone had not been the intended victim of an apparent murder attempt.

I said, "The carriage house is getting a good airing out. We'll need to find a bed for Chickie here."

She sat next to him and held both of his hands in hers. "Well, we have plenty of bedrooms, don't we, Chickie? You can have your pick of the guest rooms."

He beamed at her. "I like the one that looks out on the trees."

"You got it. And you're already in your jammies. You want to go on up now? Or would you like to watch TV with me?"

Dark eyes brightened in the unused-looking face. "Can I stay up for *The Fugitive*? Jamie always let me stay up for *The Fugitive*."

She gave him a lovely smile. "Sure, honey. Just let me get you some aspirin to go with that water, okay?"

She left to go do that, presumably from a bathroom cabinet, and I asked Chickie, "Did you have any visitors tonight?"

"I hardly ever have visitors."

"No, I mean, did anyone drop by to say hello? From the family, this evening?"

He shrugged. "Just my brother."

"Which brother?"

"Wake. He came in and watched TV with me a while."

I put my hand on his shoulder again. "Chickie, I

need you to think back. I need you to answer me very carefully. Did your brother Wake ever go near the fireplace tonight?"

"Just to turn it off before he left. He said we didn't need a fire tonight."

Walters was frowning. He got it. Like me, he knew. But he didn't say anything. Not to Chickie or to Dorena, when she returned with the aspirin bottle.

As her brother was taking the pills, I asked her, "Do you know if Wake went into the city tonight?"

She shook her head, obviously wondering why I was asking. "I don't believe so. I think he might be working out in his studio. He's got an exhibit coming up."

"Who else is home?"

"Madeline. She's in the library, reading." A tiny condescending smile twisted the coral-touched lips. "The new Harold Robbins paperback, I think. Dex is out, as usual. Likely at the Log Cabin. Why?"

"No reason. I'm just a paid snoop, remember?"

She smiled a little at that, then gathered Chickie and led him off.

When they were gone, the caretaker said, "After Wake turned that fireplace off, he turned the gas back on, didn't he, Mr. Hammer?"

"Go back down to your guardhouse, Willie," I said, ignoring the question. "Take a beer with you, if you like."

He did both those things.

* * *

The four-car garage was missing only one ride: Dex's Lincoln. The others—Wake's Jag, Dorena's Thunderbird, and Madeline's Triumph—were in their designated places. The lights in here were off, but toward the back a shaft of illumination poured through the hole in the ceiling left by the collapsible steps, which were dropped down and just waiting for me to come up.

I got out the .45.

I didn't really think Wake would be waiting for me with a gun or knife, or maybe a blunt object like whatever killed Jamison Elder. He would do the innocent bit, claiming he had shut off the fireplace in the carriage house rec room, nothing more. That he clearly remembered switching the lever to OFF.

Turning on that gas, with a flip of a lever, Wake could have increased the Dunbar inheritance pot by another million. If I hadn't found Chickie in time.

But if I accused Wake directly, and he thought I had him cold, I figured he might be capable of anything. There was something demented about all of this. Something of a madman scheming, making a murder attempt on Dex so that Abe Hazard would take the blame, faking two murder tries on himself, to arrange for his long-suffering wife to take the fall.

And a madman—a mad killer—can do almost anything. I should know.

I stood beneath the hole that was the gateway to the artist's studio above and listened. Listened.

But for a gentle night breeze at the windows, I heard not a thing. If Wake was working, wouldn't there be some sound? I didn't expect to hear a brush stroke, of course, but he'd be dabbing paint from his palette, and his chair would squeak, his sleeves would rustle as his arms moved.

Unless he wasn't *working*.

Unless he was waiting for me, the only one who might discern his crazy scheme, the renowned vigilante P.I. who'd made more self-defense murder pleas than most people get parking tickets.

I started up the steps. Slow, careful. If he wasn't making noise, I sure as hell couldn't afford to. The wood of a drop-down glorified ladder was not exactly designed to stay silent. But my gum soles helped, and I kept my eye on the glowing square above me, ready to trigger the son of a bitch to Hell if need be.

The next step was the new one, the replacement— *would it be rigged?* I checked it with the hand gripping the .45, not an easy maneuver. Seemed fine. Seemed secure. As soon as I had half-emerged, I came up the rest of the way quick, not giving a damn about noise.

His back was to me in his chair. He was in the white smock again and chinos, leaned back appraising his latest canvas, a work that seemed at first abstract but, if you looked carefully, a nude male figure could be made out. They'd love it in the Village.

"Wake," I said, approaching carefully, .45 poised to do whatever it had to. "I want you to stand up slowly.

Hands high. Turn slow and easy. Okay, pal?"

But he remained motionless.

And I knew.

Some of it was a familiar stench. Partly it was the Pollock-like splash of red spattering the canvas, not really going with the otherwise geometric nature of the design. Mostly it was the small black hole in the back of his chair.

When I came around to where I could really see him, he wasn't appraising anything but his own sudden death, his mouth and his eyes wide open, but sightless, soundless.

Had someone else stopped the madman?

Or was he just another victim?

I explored the studio, looking for clues. The State Police lab boys would give it a real once-over, but I was looking for more obvious things. Like an ejected shell, or the lack of one. The former could mean an automatic had been used, if the killer didn't collect his or her brass, and judging by the size of that bullet hole, probably a .22. The latter would mean a revolver had signed Wake Dunbar's last painting. Again, something small, a purse gun, perhaps.

And then there it was, about where an ejected shell might be: *a single plastic green button earring.*

I left it where it was, knowing I shouldn't tamper with the crime scene, but not ready to call in the official boys.

Not yet.

At the house, I checked the library to see if Madeline was still reading in there. In a cobalt-blue blouse and matching slacks, she was settled in a big, brown leather button-tufted chair, her long legs tucked up under her, a paperback in her lap (*Where Love Has Gone*) and her head drifted to one side. Her snoring was light enough to be feminine and heavy enough to be convincing.

Dorena and Chickie were still in the TV room, watching *The Fugitive*, and Dex was as usual out. And, of course, Wake was dead as hell. So I should have the upstairs to myself…

Madeline's bedroom was smaller than mine, without a private bath, though still fairly spacious. As with the rest of the house, the floor was parquet, though a light-green shag throw rug was home to a French Provincial white bed and nightstands, with matching dresser against a wall and a vanity with round mirror in one corner, each with its own similar shag. The bedspread was deeper green and plush, the pillows in their pillowcases big and fluffy. A very female room. Well, Madeline was a very female female.

I checked the closet, a walk-in affair with a lot of attractive, sexy outfits on hangers, some in the mod vein, but nothing Fifth Avenue. Her husband gave her a decent clothing allowance, it would seem, but not generous. Lots of green on display, but fabric, not folding money.

A blind man could have found the .22 automatic.

It was at the bottom of a dresser drawer filled with

frilly French-type underthings, wrapped in a sheer black negligee. A Smith & Wesson .22 Escort, a perfect little purse gun. I used the fabric of the silky garment to lift the weapon gently by its grip with forefinger and thumb and sniffed the barrel. Recently fired. I checked the five-shot clip and only four bullets remained.

This was almost certainly the gun that killed Wake.

Too easy, I thought.

At the vanity, in her jewelry box, it took about fifteen seconds to find the single plastic green button earring that just had to be the mate of the one I'd found on the art studio floor.

Too goddamn easy.

I closed the lid on the jewelry box, leaving the orphan earring right where it had been.

"Can I *help* you, Mike?" came Madeline Dunbar's voice, with an edge I'd never heard before.

I turned and said, "You're the one who needs the help. Listen to me—go back downstairs and find somewhere to sit quietly until—"

She came at me with her claws out and I slapped her, just hard enough to get her attention.

Her hand on her cheek, her big green eyes filled with rage and confusion, she stood there trembling for a moment, then slapped me back, harder than I had her.

I let her see a grin with some teeth in it. "Have we got the hysterics out of the way? Because you're going to need a friend."

Her eyes narrowed, as if trying to bring me into

focus, and she said, "What are you *talking* about?"

"Do you own a gun? A little handgun?"

The eyes widened again, her expression mingling indignation and fear. "What if I do? What does that have to do with anything?"

"Where do you keep it?"

She gestured irritably toward the nearest nightstand. "At my bedside—in case some strange man I didn't invite comes wandering in here!"

"When did you fire it last?"

Her eyes and nostrils flared. "When did I…? *What?*"

"Somebody fired it. Recently. And it's wrapped up in some lingerie, in that dresser."

Her forehead furrowed. "I… I don't understand, Mike. I don't understand *any* of this…"

I brushed red hair away from the side of her face; the ear lobe was bare and did not show any impression in the flesh indicating a clip-on earring had been there recently.

"What are you *doing*? Keep your hands off me!"

"When did you last see Wake?"

"This morning, I think! What is this *about?*"

I told her.

She stumbled over and sat on the side of her bed. Her mouth hung open and her eyes were wide and moving quickly, as if events were moving too fast and she was working to keep up.

"Either you killed Wake," I said, standing before her, "and are a very stupid girl. Or somebody is framing you. And I don't think you're stupid."

Her chin was crinkling. "Mike… will you help me?"

"I won't clean up that crime scene or this bedroom, either. You're better off letting the frame stand until somebody… maybe me… can show how some bastard or bitch fitted you for it."

Her face was blank with helplessness. "What should I do?"

"What I said before. Go find somewhere downstairs to sit and wait for the cops to show. I haven't called them yet, so you have time to think back through the evening, back through your day, and see if you can come up with anything helpful. Okay?"

She nodded. She tried to get to her feet but was unsteady, and I helped her. She was in my arms, her face lovely, her expression pitiful.

"I'm sorry I slapped you," she said.

"I'm sorry I had to slap you. Shall we go downstairs?"

We were coming down just as Dorena was guiding Chickie up to the bedroom with the view he liked. Dorena looked at Madeline and me curiously, with what might have been a hint of jealousy, and said, "Hello, you two."

I said, "Tuck him in quick and come find me."

Dorena frowned a little, but nodded, correctly reading my serious tone.

"Night, Chickie," I said.

"Night, Mike."

I used a phone in the library to call the State Police,

since we weren't within the city limits of Monticello, although I might have called the Sullivan County sheriff. But my hunch was that this was one big investigation—Wake's killing added to the now probable murders of both Chester Dunbar and Jamison Elder—and Corporal Sheridan was already familiar with the case, if not quite working it.

As it happened, Sheridan was in Monticello on another matter, and I asked the dispatcher to pass the call along to the corporal with (as this was a homicide) some urgency. That meant we wouldn't have the half hour or more wait of Sheridan driving over from his cop shop.

I was back at the Formica-top table, smoking a Lucky, when Dorena hurried in, frowning, saying, "*Here* you are. What is going *on*, Mike?"

"Have a seat," I said, and she did, and I told her about my discovery in the art studio above the garage. I did not inform her of either the lime-green earring near the corpse or the cute little .22 wrapped up in silk and lace in Madeline's dresser.

"I thought Wake tried to kill Chickie," she said numbly, staring into nothing.

"It seems like he did. But somebody killing him appears not to have anything to do with that, other than the general feeling I get that murder is in the air around here. Seems somebody in this house wants a bigger piece of the family pie."

"What are you *talking* about?"

I took smoke in, let it out. "Chickie dies, the inheritance pot gains a mil. Wake gets murdered, another mil. The killer is batting .500 tonight."

"Mike… you don't… you don't suspect *me*?"

"Who stands to gain but you or Dex or that backward boy upstairs? Or Madeline, who with Wake gone gets early access to his dough?"

"Chickie didn't try to murder himself!"

I shrugged. "Okay. So we're down to you, Dex and Madeline. And I have good reason to believe that Madeline didn't kill Wake."

"*What* good reason?"

I shook my head. "A detective has to keep a few cards to himself. But what I believe won't keep the police from hauling her sweet tail to the hoosegow tonight. She will go directly to jail and will not collect a million dollars."

Her eyes were moving quickly again. "I… I don't love Madeline, but I can't imagine she would… Mike, this is terrible. *Horrible.*"

"Could be a long night. You want me to make you some coffee?"

"Please. But why a long night?"

"The art studio and the garage itself will be considered a crime scene. And this house will be searched top to bottom."

I made the coffee. Dorena just sat there, looking shell-shocked.

It took Corporal Jim Sheridan only about fifteen

minutes to get to the Dunbar estate. I met him at the front door. He was alone but said a B.C.I. investigator and a full forensics team would be along shortly.

"Kind of a break that you were so close by," I said. We were still on the porch.

"Yeah, well," he said, "I was working that other case. The missing girls?"

"Nothing on the latest one?"

He shook his head glumly. "Nothing. Tonight I was questioning the waitresses at the All-Night Room at the Concord, to see if any of 'em saw the girl talking to somebody in the club—specifically, that guy she was seen yakking with in the parking lot. Another damn dead end."

"You'll crack it. I just wouldn't put any money on that girl still being alive."

He sighed. "Nor would I. Shall we start with the garage?"

"I'll give you the nickel tour," I said.

We detoured just briefly to take in the carriage house, where I told him of the attempted murder of Chickie Dunbar. While this would probably not be considered a crime scene, the forensics guys would check that metal fireplace for prints.

In the garage, up the ladder and into the studio, I pointed out the earring and said it belonged to the victim's wife.

"You'll soon find out," I said, "there was no love lost between her and Wake."

"Rumor has it he was a homosexual."

"I would say rumor is right. Madeline was just a front, to keep things looking respectable. But the arrangement was rubbing both of them the wrong way."

Sheridan's eyes were slits. "She sounds like our prime suspect."

I nodded. "Somewhere in here you'll find an ejected .22 shell. And when you go through her bedroom, you'll find the other lime-green earring and a little popgun that'll almost for sure be your murder weapon."

His grin had a little self-satisfied sneer in it. "So we've got her cold."

"It stinks on ice is all that's cold about it. She's no fool. She wouldn't kill her husband and serve herself up on a platter to you cops."

He was shaking his head. "That's not my judgment to make, Mike. We'll see what the B.C.I. investigators think."

They made the arrest at two-thirty-seven that morning.

CHAPTER NINE

The Monticello Courthouse, with its impressive gray stone, green trim, and grand dome, might have been erected specifically to conceal the dingy brown-brick building directly behind it. Dating back half a century or so, the blocky county jail with its eighty-nine cramped cells was not where you might expect to find a lovely redhead like Madeline Dunbar.

Yet, there she was, sitting on the edge of her brown-blanketed cot in the same cobalt-blue blouse and slacks as the night before, her face scrubbed of make-up and looking quite attractive, for a woman in Hell, anyway.

They had let me in the black-barred cell with her and I sat next to her on the cot. I presented myself as her lawyer's representative, which was true in a very sideways way: the Dunbars had, after all, hired me to investigate the suspicious deaths of their father and butler through the attorney I work with in Manhattan.

"Mike," she said, her expression tortured, her eyes wet, "I would *never* have killed Wake. I'd never kill *anyone*! But Wake… you may find it hard to buy, but I loved him, once upon a time. Loved him very much."

"That doesn't jibe with anything I've observed, honey. We both know that Wake was gay."

She winced. "But he was only… *half* gay. Or maybe three-quarters."

"You mean, his gate swung both ways?"

She nodded. "Our for-appearances-only arrangement of the last few years was something that developed… me playing the good wife while he flitted around the Village. Initially, I thought he loved me. Our sexual relationship was normal enough. He sometimes seemed to be going through the motions, but I never really suspected. Finally he told me he had someone else, and that it was a man, and when the theatrics were over, and that took weeks, we agreed to stay married."

"Why did you do that?"

Her mouth twisted. "Why do you think? For the money. With a million-dollar inheritance looming, why *not* live a lie for a few years?"

I gave her half a smile. "But you didn't, did you, doll? You found your own men to show him, and yourself, that you were still very much a desirable woman."

I might have slapped her again. She said, "Mike… that sounds so… *harsh*."

"Maybe, but all you needed to do was look in

a mirror and see what guys like me see, which is a beautiful woman."

She smiled a little. "That's better. That's not harsh at all."

I touched her hand. "What was the last straw, sugar? What sent you openly running around on Wake with every Tom and Harry's Dick?"

That got a little laugh out of her. "Well... it was Wake's own wild behavior. That guy he left me for turned out to be the first of many. My loving hubby called me a nympho! What was *he*, but the male version of that?"

"Satyr's the term. How ugly did it get between you two?"

She shrugged. "There were occasional fights, but only arguing, never anything physical. I wouldn't have minded him getting a little rough... oh, I know that sounds terrible, but it maybe would have meant he still cared, a little."

She began to cry. She had a box of tissues ready for that.

I held her hand till she got hold of herself, then when she did, I squeezed a little.

"Here's the problem," I told her. "Everything you've told me about your relationship with Wake... while it's very compelling, even moving... doesn't help your situation."

"But..."

"I have to be harsh again, honey. That you once

loved him, and were spurned... particularly thrown over for a man... has murder motive written all over it."

Her face took on a terrible blankness. "My God," she said quietly. "It *does*, doesn't it?"

"That saying about the truth shall set you free? Doesn't apply here."

Her eyes grew huge and her mouth became a contorted thing. "But I *didn't* kill him! I swear I didn't!"

"I believe you. I've seen many a frame in my time, but never one more obvious than what you were fitted for. It may be that the cops'll be smart enough to see through it... but we can't count on that."

The wet eyes suddenly had hope in them. "You *do* believe me. You... you're going to *help* me?"

"I said you needed a friend. Well, you've got one. We'll start with lining you up with the attorney I work with back in Manhattan."

"What about Mr. Hines?"

I shook my head. "He's not a criminal lawyer and, anyway, I'm not sure where his loyalties lie. You're a Dunbar, yeah, but only by marriage. And the biggest suspect in this thing is a longtime client of his— Dexter Dunbar."

She frowned in thought. "You suspect Dex? Why not Dorena?"

"She's a possibility, and so is the kid Chickie, if he's been sandbagging us. But Dex is a man with real money trouble, and a thirst for getting into more of it. You as Wake's murderer takes you out of the inheritance picture and tosses another million into the Dunbar pot. That could be mighty tempting to somebody in Dex's straits. And he has complete access to the estate—the art studio and your bedroom, for example. He would know about your gun. He would know where to find your jewelry box to plant an earring."

She was shaking her head a little; it was all coming at her very fast. "Mike... what should I do?"

"Nothing. Sit tight. Clam up. You haven't given a statement yet, have you?"

"No. I haven't said *anything*... just that I'm innocent."

"Well, that never hurts." Never did any good, either. "You tell them they'll be hearing from your lawyer, and that he's in Manhattan, so it may take a while. No harm in buying a little time."

"Time I spend in *here*," she pointed out.

"Tough it out. I intend to clear you of this, fast. With a little luck, you won't have to spend more than a day or two behind bars."

Her smile was a pleasure to see. "You're wonderful."

I got to my feet. "I hear that from dames all the time."

"You're funny. You talk like *Guys and Dolls*."

"Sweetie, *Guys and Dolls* talks like me."

Outside the jail in the parking lot, Corporal Jim Sheridan, in an echo of the first time I saw him, was leaning against his black-and-white having a smoke. He looked as crisp and cool as the morning in his gray uniform and purple-banded Stetson. He had on the sunglasses again, too.

As I ambled over, he said, "How'd it go with your client?"

I smirked as I lit up a Lucky. "You know I can't tell you that, Jim. But thanks for greasing the wheels some so I could get to her."

His sunglasses lenses reflected me back at myself. "You really think she's innocent, Mike?"

That was worth another smirk. "She's not innocent, not with *that* shape... but she's no murderer."

His expression was weak for such a square-jawed face. "I grant you she was sloppy about it, but she may have lost her head and—"

"No. If she did it, and she didn't, it had to be very damn premeditated. Madeline Dunbar had to take that gun out of her nightstand drawer and walk outside and over to the garage and climb those fold-down steps, maybe having to yank the cord to bring them down herself, all of which is plenty of time to cool off, but no, she goes up there and shoots her husband in the back, cool as you please, yet somehow manages to lose her earring, leave a shell casing behind, and then go back to her room and hide her gun away in a sublimely stupid fashion. Balls."

"I won't say I don't see your point. But murderers are people, and people don't always act rationally."

"I'll write that down." I took smoke in, let it out. "So what's your involvement now? B.C.I. will be taking over, right?"

He nodded. "I'm just support now. The local gendarme. This B.C.I. guy Bullard, Mike… you met him last night?"

"Briefly. A charmer."

A shrug. "He's good at what he does, but he's a hard-nosed bastard. Some might even say he's an asshole. Just a word to the wise."

"Should be sufficient," I said lightly. I nodded toward a figure walking across the parking lot toward us. "Who's this freight train?"

"Oh, hell," Sheridan said very softly. "It's that Linda's father."

"Who's Linda?"

"Our most recent missing girl."

He was a small, bespectacled, mustached man about fifty in a dark, indifferently tailored brown suit, a lighter brown tie flapping. He was barreling right toward us with an expression of unmistakable angry frustration.

"*Corporal Sheridan! Corporal Sheridan!*"

The trooper smiled in a polite way but didn't reply until the little man had planted himself before us. "Mr. Cohen," he said with a nod.

Mr. Cohen was trembling, and displeasure quavered in his voice. "I don't know whether I'm lucky or not, running into you. I'm here to see the sheriff, to see if *he* might have any advice for Linda's mother and me, besides what you seem to be recommending, which is sit on our damn hands."

Sheridan held up a palm. "Mr. Cohen, we *are*

investigating. We're looking for your daughter. Nothing new yet. You'll be my first call."

Cohen barely seemed to be listening. "I've been asking around. It turns out that Linda isn't the *first* girl to disappear under mysterious circumstances on your watch. What do you have to say for yourself about that?"

"I understand how you feel, sir. But we are—"

"Understand how I feel? You understand how I feel? You understand how it feels to wonder if some lunatic has grabbed your daughter and is maybe, maybe *raping* her right now? Or maybe she's dead in a ditch or an accident victim unidentified in some hospital, and you people… you people…"

He lowered his head and began to weep. His chest had been heaving some, from rushing over to us, but now it was heaving even more with his sobbing. The sound of it was awful: that combination of rage and sorrow unique to a parent with a missing child.

Sheridan reached out to the man, as if to touch his shoulder supportively, but stopped short. It would have been an intrusion.

The little man was snorting snot now, and muttering over and over, "Sorry… sorry… I'm sorry… you're doing… doing the best you can. *Please keep trying!* Please keep trying!"

"We will, sir."

Cohen seemed to notice me for the first time. He said, "I *know* you, don't I?"

"I don't believe we've met, sir," I said.

"*I know you!* You're Mike Hammer! You're the one who… you used to be in the papers all the time!"

I gave him a small smile. "I used to be a lot of things."

"You're still a private detective?"

"Still a private detective."

Sheridan forgotten now, the tortured little father positioned himself before me and said, "Will *you* take Linda's case? Maybe you can clear away the red tape and really dig into this. You have a reputation for—"

"Mr. Cohen," I said. "I'm on a case up here already. But if you don't get satisfaction from the State Police, call me in a few days at my office. I should have this other matter wrapped up by then."

He swallowed, nodded, offered me his hand. I shook it. His grasp was firm with desperation.

"I'll do that, Mr. Hammer. Thank you. Thank you!" He glanced at Sheridan. "Corporal," he said dismissively.

Then he went into the jail for his meeting with the sheriff.

"You're pretty sure of yourself," Sheridan said. "Gonna wrap your case up in a few days, huh?"

I gave him a nice, nasty grin with plenty of teeth.

"Watch me," I said.

Its red neon sign burning bright in the night, Honest Abe's Log Cabin was doing land-office business. But then this was Friday at nine p.m., and it would be. The parking lot was packed, and I was lucky to find a place to squeeze the Galaxie into. I was alone tonight, or almost alone—my .45 was along for the ride.

I had spent the afternoon interviewing the Dunbar staff—Dixie the cook, Lena the maid, and the three-woman cleaning staff, in for one of their twice-a-week stints. I conducted all of the interviews in the kitchen at the Formica-topped table, where I also sat Willie Walters down for a talk. What I was after was anything out of the ordinary that any of them might have witnessed, particularly arguments between the Dunbar siblings.

While the help confirmed that there was no love lost between the two brothers and their half-sister, the three Dunbars mostly expressed their lack of interest by ignoring each other. I already knew that Dixie was damn near a short-order cook, rustling up grub on the fly for each of them morning, noon, and night. As for Chickie, Dixie and the rest found him quiet and odd—not exactly world-shattering observations—but had never witnessed anything untoward between him and his sibs.

"Miss Dorena really likes the poor child," Dixie said. "That's easy enough to see. Mr. Wake pretty much looked right through him, and Mr. Dex just seems to find him an annoyance. Not that they see much of him—the boy comes over from the carriage house for breakfast and supper only, and like I said, the Dunbars don't often eat together."

None of it was very helpful.

Willie Walters did offer one thing of interest. He confirmed that it was unusual for Wake to go watch television with Chickie, as he had last night.

"Wake weren't real big on brotherly love," the caretaker said.

That suggested Wake was there to fill that room and Chickie's lungs with gas. Could it be coincidental that just after he tried to kill his half-brother, he got himself murdered as well? By another sibling?

I handed my hat to the girl behind the check stand—again, no need for the trenchcoat in the almost spring weather—and entered the bustling, smoky casino. Thugs in tuxes were threading through, keeping an eye on things, as before. I found Dex once again at his favorite blackjack table, where he was giving lessons on how to stink up the joint while cowgirl waitresses brought him one tumbler of bourbon and water after another.

He looked terrible, the circles under his eyes as dark as his short but untended hair; he hadn't bothered with a tie or an ascot, either, just a light-blue polo shirt under a perfect-looking navy blazer that only emphasized what a mess he was otherwise.

Unless she was in the restaurant bar picking up some lucky stranger, Brenda Something was not in attendance tonight. Apparently, like me, Dex was going stag. I stood nearby, but not crowding him, and gave him a nod. He flicked a sour look my way; that was it for a greeting.

I watched him lose a grand in fifteen minutes, and then he got up abruptly and got almost nose-to-nose with me. He was trembling, as if trying to hold back rage.

"We need to talk," he said.

The times in my life where that sentence was followed by something positive aren't worth noting. Of course, it was usually a female saying it.

"Happy to," I said with a smile.

In a rush, he led me outside and just to the left of the entry. Busy as the Log Cabin was, out here it was quiet, everybody already inside as if in the middle of a church service. I could smell the bourbon on him, but with these gentleman-drinker types, it's hard to tell how drunk they really are. In any case, he had an exposed-nerve manner, half-furious, half-frightened, his eyes shifting in a search for words.

So I took the lead.

"You have a funny kind of way," I said, lighting up a Lucky, "of grieving for your brother."

"What business is it of yours, Hammer?"

"Well, when there's been a murder… or two or three… I like to keep track of the reactions of individuals involved. I know your sister was at a Monticello funeral parlor this afternoon, making the sad arrangements. I offered to go along, in case she wanted her hand held. She declined, graciously, but declined. Were you there with her, Dex? Lending support?"

His face tightened defensively. "I had business that needed taking care of."

"Yeah, I saw how frantic it gets for you at the office. But here I am, going on and on, and you're the one who wanted to talk. So talk."

His upper lip curled and showed me some capped teeth. "You're an arrogant son of a bitch."

"I've been called way worse, Dex. You'll have to try harder than that."

His chin went up. "How about this? You're *fired*, Hammer. The Dunbar family has no further need, no further use for your services. Send a bill and we'll settle up. In the meantime, I want you out of our house, tonight."

"You didn't hire me. Your sister did."

His eyes flared. "I'm the head of the family, and I say you're dismissed! Hell, you barge in bragging that you'll find out who killed my father and our butler, when those deaths have been declared accidental, and then, right under your nose, Wake really *is* murdered. Not to mention that someone tried to kill Chickie!"

"That 'someone' seems to have been Wake."

"If so, I'm prepared to leave it to the police to sort out."

"What about your concerns for your own life? Those gunshots outside your office? Your belief that Abe Hazard was behind it?"

Too lightly, he said, "Everything between Abe and me is settled. We've drawn up a new agreement and I've signed it and so has he."

"Gambling debts can't legally be collected in this state, you know."

"Maybe not, but I have a, uh… moral obligation."

I exhaled smoke, chuckling as I did. "You're one hell of a piece of work, Dexter. You think Hazard tried to kill you, or at least had his boys throw a dangerous scare into you, and yet you still come here and gamble. You still do business with him. And let me define 'moral obligation' for you—if you don't pay up, the New York boys will come calling."

He showed me what he thought was a smile. "I don't give a damn what you think, Hammer. I just want you *gone*."

Then *he* was gone, heading quickly back inside.

I finished my smoke, enjoying the crisp mountain air, yet somehow longing for Manhattan and all those sweet exhaust fumes.

Back in the casino, I headed over to the bar at the left. This was mostly a station for giving the little cowgirl waitresses fresh free drinks for gamblers, but half a dozen stools were lined up, only a couple taken. I edged my posterior up onto one that was two away from the nearest patron.

The bartenderess was a tall, well-built gal with shoulder-length raven hair and a fashion-defying pageboy. She was in the same Hollywood-western attire as the waitresses, right down to the cowgirl hat. She sauntered over to take my drink order and looked right at me with big dark eyes in a face whose features were both well-carved and beautiful.

I said, "Hi, Velda."

"Mike. Four Roses and ginger?"

"Maybe just beer for now. What've you got on tap?"

"That you'd put up with? Blue Ribbon."

"Do it."

She filled a pilsner and brought it over. None of the waitresses were hounding her for drinks at the moment, and the other two guys at the bar were nursing their own beers, possibly contemplating what to tell the little woman about their big losses.

"I'm impressed," I said. "I expected you to be out there slinging drinks to suckers."

"I have mixology skills," she said, "as you well know. And they needed a bartender. Tips aren't wonderful, though. Girls on the floor do much better. Where did you and Dex Dunbar go off to?"

"We just stepped out so he could fire me."

An eyebrow arched. "Well, at least *I'm* gainfully employed."

"He didn't hire me. Dorena did."

Her smile was a pretty twitch. "Ah, the lovely Dorena. I don't see her with you tonight."

"She has a dead half-brother to mourn for. And has to mourn twice as hard because Dex's idea of grieving is to give more money to Abe Hazard."

"That's who hired me. Abe Hazard. Slick character."

One of the other patrons at the bar was ready for another beer. She got it for him, then returned.

"I'm off in half an hour," she said. "Meet me outside where we can really talk."

I nodded and finished the beer, as two cowgirls came up with drink orders to be filled.

For a while I killed time playing a nickel slot machine. I hit pretty good and one of the cowgirls traded me a roll of quarters for a brimming tray of nickels.

I was just slipping the ten bucks in coin into my sportscoat pocket when Abe Hazard came waddling over, a big smile blossoming on his Lincoln-bearded face. That weird squat build of his guaranteed the tux was custom.

He smiled chummily and put a hand on my arm, leaning close. "What's Mike Hammer doing, playing the nickel slots? That's just for the blue-hair broads."

"I told you before, Abe. I'm not a gambler."

"Maybe not, Mike. But a card. A real card."

He patted me on the back, and went back to glad-handing his Friday night crowd. Odd-looking duck, that movie-star handsome mug stuck onto a Macy's Thanksgiving Parade hot-air balloon.

I was enjoying the cool, pine-scented night, working my way through another Lucky, when Velda came out, looking sexy as hell in the short, fringed cowgirl skirt. She had left the hat behind, however, and her expression was no-nonsense. If I was hoping for "Ride 'em, cowboy," it would have to be another night.

She led me around the side of the building. A kitchen exhaust fan down from us was wheezing and rattling.

"Mike," she said, "according to the other girls, this place is a gaff joint—I've been warned not to gamble here. The roulette wheels are rigged, the dice are weighted, the blackjack dealers are mechanics."

"Nobody has to deal bottom cards to Dex Dunbar," I said. "He's lousy without any help. Vel, I think your first night at Honest Abe's is going to be your last— especially since the tips are so lousy."

"Do we or don't we have a client?"

"Even if Dorena and Dex hand me my walking papers, I still have that buck Pat gave me. He's my real client here, though without the Dunbar family's cooperation, it'll be tricky as hell."

She nodded. "Well, Dex was around here all afternoon, mostly in Hazard's office. The Cabin opens at four, and I came in at two, for the floor manager to give me the routine. Dex came in shortly after that. Hazard was acting real chummy."

"God knows what kind of document Abe talked him into signing."

They came from both sides, not rushing us or anything, just lumbering toward us, two from around front of the building, two more from around back. I recognized them all—they were floorwalkers, bouncers, from inside… apes in monkey suits. Nobody had a weapon in his hands, though the hands themselves were weapons, poised to grab, fingers curled. I went for the .45 but thick arms looped around me, pinning me. One of them had Velda, too, one arm around her waist, the other grabbing a handful of that raven hair and yanking her back, exposing her throat to the night as if he were a vampire, not a hood.

Of the two facing us, the out-front one was the big sloped-brow, butch-haircut bastard with the little flecks of white scar on his cheeks and across the bridge of his flat nose. He swung a fist into my belly and I bent over as much as I could with my arms held back as they were.

"Mr. Hazard says you're not welcome here," he said. His voice was a little higher-pitched than you'd expect from that Buick of a body, and he worked a little too hard to sound tough. "We're gonna give you a reminder so you don't forget."

I ignored him, looking over at Velda and the brute behind her, yanking her back by the hair. He had a small, slightly pointy head despite his huge frame, and his eyes were stupid.

"Don't," I advised him.

"You're funny," the brute said. He had the deep voice that went with his body, if not the pointed head.

The butch boy slipped his thick hand under my sportscoat and yanked out the .45. Then, gloating, he shoved the rod in his waistband, the tux jacket unbuttoned.

It never feels good to get smacked in the belly, but I'd been right about the butch boy—he, like all these assholes, was too muscle-bound to really be a problem. What they had on us was size, numbers, and of course surprise.

I stomped hard on the toes of the guy behind me and his arms popped open, releasing me. I didn't bother turning to see what he looked like—I knew about where his balls would be, and I sent an elbow looking for them. The scream was high-pitched and feminine, which is ironic if you think about it, and butch boy was frozen for a second, just a second, but that was long enough for me to slip my hand into my pocket and bring back the roll of quarters, which were neatly tucked into my fist when I hit him in the mouth. The quarters went flying and so did four or five of his teeth.

The cowgirls at Honest Abe's wore spike-heel leather boots, which was what Velda was in, and her pointed stomp was aimed at the ankle of the guy behind her, not his toes. His arms released her reflexively, and she swung around and threw a hard fist into his Adam's apple. He was clutching his throat, wobbling, when she kneed him in the balls, and then both of our come-from-behind assailants were down, writhing in pain. I kicked mine in the head and he stopped writhing.

Meanwhile, butch boy was on his knees, spitting out shards of tooth through foamy red. I reached down and got my .45 out of his waistband and slapped him with it—should leave the whitest scar of all among the flecks. He took a nap. The goon in the tux behind him was going for a gun and I shot him in the leg, the thigh, toppling him. The sound thundered in the night, but the kitchen exhaust played silencer. I stepped around butch boy, who was choking on his own blood, and plucked the gun from under the arm of the tuxedo goon and tossed it off into the thicket hugging the pines.

I disarmed the guy who'd grabbed me from behind—he was unconscious from my kicking him in the head—and tossed his gun into the brush, too. The guy who'd grabbed Velda and got his nuts crushed for his trouble was on his side, kind of in a fetal position, his back a target for Velda—who was kicking him there repeatedly—eliciting little cries of pain. He had a .38 Police Special on his hip, which I collected and tossed. She kept kicking him.

"They've had enough fun," I said, taking her by the arm and walking her away. She was breathing a little hard, but then so was I. I suggested she gather her things and wait for me at her car, and she nodded. She didn't have to be told I had things to do.

Nobody was on guard outside Abe Hazard's office—not surprising, since the first team bouncers had been sent to deal with Velda and me.

I came in fast and slammed the door behind me so hard Hazard jumped in his desk chair, almost goddamn bounced. He got a desk drawer open and was scrambling for a gun when I slammed it shut on him. His scream was a whiny little embarrassment. Then I dragged him off the chair and dumped him on the floor.

I looked down on him in every sense. "You recognized Velda, didn't you, Abe?"

He didn't say anything. The handsome, bearded face on the balloon body was clenched in terror.

I said, "She's made the papers, too, from time to time. That was my bad judgment. That's on me, not you. But guess what? You pay anyway."

I yanked him to his feet, which, as much as he weighed, was doing something, and with one hand holding onto the front of his tux, I started slapping him with the other. When bloody drool was leaking out the corners of his mouth, I paused to pose a question.

"You have Dexter Dunbar's new agreement in that file cabinet over there?"

He swallowed hard and nodded.

"All copies?"

He nodded.

"How many?"

"The… the original… and two carbons."

"I'm gonna let you walk over there and get them."

He nodded.

"Can you do that without my help, Abe?"

He nodded.

I let go of him and he staggered over to the file cabinet.

As he was just about to pull open the top drawer, I said, "Here's an idea. If you have a gun hidden in there, make a play. I would be interested to know how many slugs it would take for a rhino like you to go down."

He even nodded at that.

His fireplace was going, and that was the perfect place to get rid of the documents. We were leaning over into its warmth when he got the nerve to say, "Are you crazy, Hammer? Do you know who I'm connected to?"

"The Evello bunch," I said. "Be sure to ask them if they want to tangle with Mike Hammer over something as chickenshit as Dexter Dunbar's gambling losses."

He had no comment.

"As of right now," I said, "you're banning Dexter Dunbar from this place. He'll probably find somewhere else to gamble, but maybe it'll be at a straight house."

I helped him over to his desk, taking time to remove the little .32 from the desk drawer and drop the weapon in my pocket. I told him to call a doctor, a discreet one.

"I... I don't need a damn doctor," he said, gathering what shreds of his pride remained.

"That's up to you," I said, at the door. "But I shot one of your boys in the leg, and the others are in various states of disrepair."

He was staring at the phone as if waiting for it to dial itself when I went out.

CHAPTER TEN

Velda was checked in at the Laurels Motel and Country Club on Sackett Lake, four miles southwest of Monticello. I considered shooing her back to the city, but decided to keep her close at hand.

Tonight I would stay by her, in case there was any blowback from my Log Cabin visit. She'd listed the motel phone number when filling out her job application there, so a little paranoia was called for.

And just in case Hazard's Evello connection might inspire Manhattan retaliation, I gave Pat a quick call and suggested he have a watch put on the apartment building where she and I each had pads.

Think what you like, but I spent most of the night in that yellow-and-turquoise motel room in a chair with the .45 in my lap, eyes glued on the door, kept company by Jean Shepherd and other late-night radio, at low volume. And when I did stretch out on one of two twin beds, it was to catch some Zs while Velda took her turn in the chair with her Baby Browning .25. That's the way she was—still in the cute cowgirl outfit—when I woke up just after nine a.m.

After a shower and a beauty regimen she didn't really need, Velda changed into a powder-blue blouse and darker blue mini, which the Log Cabin spike-heel boots set off nicely. As for me, I'd need to get back to the Dunbar place to drag a razor across my face and trade in my rumpled clothes for something presentable.

For now, though, I just tugged on my hat, and Velda and I headed over to the motel coffee shop for some breakfast. Laurels, not quite on a scale with such other Catskills resorts as Kutsher's and the Concord, was nonetheless a sprawling fifties-modern place with indoor and (not in use just yet) outdoor pools.

In a turquoise vinyl booth, each side like the back seat of a '57 Chevy, I scarfed down a lox-and-onion omelet while figure-conscious Velda settled for a fruit cup. Over coffee, we discussed our situation.

"Hold onto that room," I said. "I may need it to work out of. Might lose my sleeping privileges at the Dunbar place if Dex holds any sway."

"What about our buddy Abe Hazard?" she asked.

"He would've come at us last night," I said, shrugging it off. "By now he figures you've booked it back to Manhattan. No, I put a scare into him and that's that. What name are you registered under?"

"Wilma Wykowski."

I swallowed a bit of bagel and grinned at her. "You sure don't look like a Wilma."

Velda gave me half a smirk and one raised eyebrow. "You should've seen her. Wilma Wykowski and I worked Vice together, and was *she* a knockout." She heaved a sigh, which challenged the powder-blue blouse. "So… I'll just nap and watch TV and stay at your beck and call. But what's on *your* program?"

A waitress in pink and white came over and refilled our coffee.

When she was gone, I said, "I'm going to see whether Dorena Dunbar agrees with her stepbrother that I'm off the payroll. At some point I'll track Dex down and let him know, if he doesn't already, that he's out of debt with Hazard but also persona non grata at the Log Cabin. And I'm hoping to get hold of that lawyer, Hines, again. I have a few dozen more questions for the good counselor."

Velda frowned over her coffee cup. "Mike, you really think Madeline Dunbar was framed? You know, if killing Wake was a spur of the moment thing, she might just have acted, well… stupidly. She might've simply lost that earring, and also panicked and hid that gun away in her drawer, intending to get rid of it later."

I shook my head. "No, Madeline was framed all right. She's anything but stupid, even under stress. What nags at me is the notion that Wake tried to kill that grown kid Chickie and then turned around and got himself murdered, the same damn night."

She smirked. "Seems like murder is catching around here."

"Yeah, but it's not the damn flu. Sure, there's plenty of money at stake, but… doll, I can feel *something* going on. There's a homicidal hand behind all of this. And it's not some gangster like Abe Hazard, or some gold-digger-in-over-her-head like Madeline Dunbar."

"*Who*, Mike?"

I shrugged, sipped coffee, said, "I don't know. That's a family with more skeletons than closets. But whoever it is, I promise you one thing—I'll get 'em looking down the barrel of my .45 before this thing is over."

Her lips pursed into a smile. "You're so cute, sometimes."

I didn't roll into the Dunbar estate till almost ten o'clock, and half an hour later—after the bathroom rituals and getting into a fresh suit—I found Dorena and Chickie at the big dining room table having a late breakfast. As before, Chickie was down at the far end, working on his *New York Times* crossword puzzle. Today his kiddie western-style shirt was pink with metal buttons and the usual Lone Ranger patch on the breast pocket.

Two chairs down from him sat Dorena, her make-up typically light with her trademark coral lipstick, her blonde hair back in a short ponytail, her blouse light yellow and short-sleeved, her denim pedal pushers looking crisp and new. These, I learned later, were her work togs.

I sat across from her, after risking Dixie taking offense when she heard I'd already had breakfast. Dorena, eating light—toast and a poached egg— looked at me with alarm and some irritation.

"Where were you last night?" she demanded in an oddly hurt tone.

I gave her a sheepish grin. "And here I thought I was of age."

That embarrassed her. "Sorry. I don't have a right to…"

"Sure you do. I should have let you know, and would have, but by the time I knew I wouldn't make it back, it was too late to call."

Her cheeks were flushed. "I shouldn't have said anything. I'm sorry…"

"Stop it. My fault entirely. But frankly, I didn't know if I'd still be welcome."

Her eyebrows narrowed but her eyes widened. "Why on earth not?"

"I had something of a run-in with Dex last night. At the Log Cabin. My apologies for leaving you behind."

She nodded, her expression pained now. "I've had my fill of that place."

I turned a hand over. "Dex feels I'm interfering with his right to throw his inheritance away. He fired me last night—said the Dunbars would no longer require my services."

Down at the other end of the table, Chickie was hunkered over the crossword, working furiously.

"That's ridiculous," Dorena said, some cold anger in her voice. "He had no right to do that. You aren't working for the family; you're working for *me*."

"That's how I viewed it. But perhaps I shouldn't stay on here—sleeping at the house, I mean. Dex is pretty hostile, and it'll only be worse when he finds out I closed out his account at the Log Cabin."

"How do you mean?"

"I mean the boss there tore up your stepbrother's I.O.U.s and also agreed to ban him from the club. I doubt Dex will take the latter kindly."

She rushed around the table and came over and hugged me, her standing, me sitting. "You are *wonderful*. So wonderful!"

"Four out of five housewives agree," I said.

"Don'tworryaboutDex.I'llhandlehim.Hedidn'tmake it home last night, either. Probably went home with that Brenda person."

He probably hadn't, but I didn't get into that. The way he'd been tying one on, he might be asleep in his Lincoln in the Log Cabin parking lot for all I knew.

She sat in the chair next to me. "So what now? What next?"

"I want a look at your father's will, and I'd like to have a copy made that I can show the attorney I work with back in the city. Hines has been somewhat cooperative, but I still don't have the full picture.

Would you help me make that happen?"

She shrugged a little. "Well, of course. If I can. I believe he's in the office on Saturday mornings. You should be able to catch him there. It's getting late enough, though, that you should call him. Don't want to miss him."

"I don't," I agreed.

She provided me with the number, and I used the phone on the kitchen wall while she returned to the dining room table and her skimpy breakfast, and the company of a precocious man/child in the process of beating the *New York Times* at its own game.

Hines himself answered, on the second ring, but I'd barely begun when he cut me off, dripping condescension.

"Mr. Hammer, you must understand that we've been using the term 'will' loosely. What Chester Dunbar put in place is more properly termed a living trust. He did this during his lifetime and set me up as the trustee."

I'd run into this before. "Which means his financial affairs are kept out of the public record."

And away from me, if executor Hines wished.

"That's right," Hines said. "Mr. Dunbar knew, with his heart condition, that he might be incapacitated or worse. And like many wealthy people, he wanted to control what happened to his property after his death."

Specifically, through the trust-fund arrangements for his offspring.

I said, patiently, "I'd like to see the living trust documents. And I may want copies to show the attorney my agency works with."

He chuckled softly in my ear. "I'm afraid that's entirely up to my discretion, Mr. Hammer."

I gave the receiver a dirty look. "I can put Dorena Dunbar on the line and she can give her approval. Or she can put it in writing again, if you'd prefer."

Now his voice took on an irritating aloofness. "Although I *do* represent the estate, Miss Dunbar is not technically my client."

"Who *is* your client, Mr. Hines?"

"Chester Dunbar, of course. And I doubt you can obtain *his* permission."

Shakespeare was right about the lawyers.

"But I tell you what, Mr. Hammer," he said placatingly. "Come to my office this afternoon, right after lunch—one o'clock, say? And I will deal with any questions you might still have… and I can judge, on a case-by-case basis, if answering would seem to be in the best interest of the estate."

I made the appointment and hung up.

I returned to the dining room table, sitting next to Dorena, and filled her in on the conversation.

Frowning in concern, she asked, "Do you suspect Mr. Hines of anything untoward?"

"With the kind of money at stake here, I suspect everybody but myself. And I'm keeping a close eye on me."

That made her smile a little, but concern kept her brow tight.

Changing the subject, I asked, "Working today? Giving Lillian What's-Her-Name a run for her money?"

She nodded. "I'm starting the third act. It's a modern-day retelling of *King Lear*."

"So," I said, "not a musical, then?"

That got a very nice smile out of her. "No, not a musical…"

"Oh," I said, "I'll need the address of Hines & Carroll…"

Her eyebrows went up. "Didn't you know? Their offices are right above Dex's on Main."

"Small world," I said.

Maybe a little too small.

"*Done!*" Chickie blurted, pencil tossed, hands high in victory.

I whispered to Dorena, "What does Chickie know about Wake?"

Sotto voce, she said, "Just that he died. No details. And certainly nothing about Wake's attempt on… you know."

I nodded.

Chickie backed up his chair, its legs scraping like fingernails on a blackboard, and got to his feet. He looked at me with that boyish face blue with beard and said, "Walk me back, Mike?"

"Sure, champ."

So once again, I walked him back, over the fieldstone path, his hand in mine, tight. The ground was getting soft and messy, hardly any patches of snow left. He was being careful to stay on the stones.

Right when we got to the side door leading into the carriage house rec room, he looked at me with childish directness and said, "Is Wake in heaven, too? Like Mr. Elder?"

"Sure he is."

"Is heaven crowded?"

Not as crowded as Hell.

"No," I said, "there's plenty of room for Wake and Mr. Elder both. And your dad, too. Do you remember your dad?"

His brow knit just slightly. "I guess. I can't see his face any more. Why do people's faces disappear in your head after they die?"

"They don't always. Do you have a picture of him?"

"No. Could I get one?"

"I'm sure your sister would give you one, if you asked her. That would help you remember him."

"Thanks, Mike."

Then he gave me a hug and slipped inside.

I parked on the street just down from Dexter's Financial Services, where a door between it and the adjacent business led to a tiny alcove with a flight of narrow stairs yawning before me. I went up to a small landing—the building was only two stories—and went through the HINES & CARROLL LAW OFFICES door into an empty outer office. Nothing fancy, but not shabby—

half a dozen chairs, a table of old magazines, an empty reception desk.

This was Saturday morning and apparently nobody was working but Hines. To confirm this I took the liberty of peeking into the office whose door said LEONARD CARROLL, PRIVATE. Nobody at that desk, either.

I knocked at the similar door saying CLARENCE HINES, PRIVATE, and announced myself.

No answer.

I went in and almost stumbled over him—not Hines, but Dexter Dunbar. Still in last night's now-not-so-crisp blazer, he was in a heap, face down, with a .38 Colt Cobra in his right hand—not in a tight grip, more a caress. Breathing but otherwise not making a move or a sound, he lay with his head near the door, his feet at the edge of a throw rug that covered much of the wooden floor, the fabric bunched up. I knelt to examine the damp spot on the back of his head and my fingers found a decent-sized lump.

The poor bastard had been bashed a good one from behind.

In front of me, perched on that throw rug, was a big, oak file-folder-stacked desk with phone and family photos, but no one sitting there; at left a wall of law books and at right a row of file cabinets. From where I stood, no chair was visible behind the desk, so I went around for a closer look.

Hines was on the floor and so was his chair, both of them toppled by a gunshot, though only the attorney had been hit. His head and body were tilted slightly to my left and he was staring past me with three eyes, two that used to see and another that was a black hole between, welling a teardrop of blood.

I knelt and felt the attorney's throat, not checking for a pulse—not with that bullet hole in the head—but for body warmth. There was some. The glop of blood and brains that had splashed onto the headrest of the fallen chair glistened.

This was a fairly fresh corpse.

With .45 in hand, I made sure I was alone but for Dex and the dead man, searching the place, including the closets in the outer office and those of both attorneys; there were men's and ladies' rooms to check, too, down a hallway between the two legal offices. It led to a rear exit and wooden steps down to a graveled parking recession between buildings. Nobody on the little porch and no sign of anyone below.

Dex was starting to come around; the way he was moaning, he had a headache going that would top any of his many hangovers.

With a handkerchief, I plucked the .38 from his flaccid fingers, then helped him into a sitting position there on the floor. While he collected himself, I sniffed the gun barrel—recently fired.

He squinted at me through his head pain. "Hammer... what... what the hell... Why are *you* here?"

"Let's start with what *you're* doing here, Dex."

For someone who had just woken up, he looked

like he might fall asleep any moment, eyelids droopy, head weaving. "Hines called down... called down and asked me to come up here. He had something important... something important he wanted to discuss. Didn't say what."

"You're *sure* it was Hines? Could it have been someone trying to sound like him?"

He started to shake his head, then thought better of it. "No, no, it was him, all right. I was downstairs in my office, sacked out on the couch."

"When was this?"

He checked his watch. "Not... not ten minutes ago."

I showed him the Colt Cobra in the handkerchief in my palm. "Does this look familiar?"

"Yes! Christ. It's mine. I keep it in my glove compartment. But I, uh, don't have a license for it. What are you doing with it?"

I slipped it in my suitcoat pocket. "Well, it was in your hand when I found you asleep here on the floor. Let me help you up. There's something... *somebody*... you should see."

I did that, and when he saw the dead attorney sprawled behind the desk next to the toppled chair, he whitened and his mouth dropped open like a trap door.

"If you're going to puke," I said, "use one of the johns out there."

He held up a quavering palm. "No... no. I'll be all right."

I walked him over to a black leather couch just inside

the door. He sat hunched, hands on his thighs, eyes on the floor. "Hammer... you don't... think... think—"

"That you did this?" I sat next to him. "No. Not with that knot on the back of your skull. But try to get past the cops with that, and they'll just say you slipped on that rug trying to get out, cracked your head and rolled over while you were not quite as dead to the world as Hines here."

He seemed on the verge of bawling. "I didn't have any *reason* to... to kill him."

"Oh, they'll dig one up. Like for starters, maybe you being unhappy that the executor of your father's living trust didn't want to advance you any money."

I've had eyes look at me sadder, but they belonged to a basset hound. "What am I going to do, Mr. Hammer?"

"Oh, are you my client again?"

His hands were clasped, begging, praying. "I'm sorry about last night... so sorry. And I *know* you got my debts voided. I owe you so much!"

"Skip it," I said. I didn't think I could take it if he started thanking me for getting him banned at that clip joint. "Do you want to turn yourself in?"

"No! Hell, no! But... what *choice* do I have?"

I gestured vaguely. "Since nobody has rushed in here to see about the gunshot—these non-commercial businesses and the offices above them must be pretty much empty on Saturday—you have options."

"Options! What the hell kind of—"

"Somebody tried to frame you, just like somebody

THE WILL TO KILL

tried to frame your sister-in-law Madeline. I wouldn't say whoever it is has much finesse, but he or she is goddamn determined. I would suggest you let me salt you away somewhere while I sort this the hell out. My secretary is in town—you may remember her, she was working the bar last night at your favorite haunt—and I can call and have her pick you up. We have a room out at the Laurels. Live on room service and keep a low profile for a while."

"We just… just walk away from this?"

"You walk away, in the protective custody of my secretary, who is also a partner in my agency, an armed and licensed private detective."

Something approaching hope was flickering in the frantic eyes. "What will *you* do?"

"I'll call the State Police and tell them I found the body. I can't let you get rid of the gun—it's the murder weapon, and you may have some explaining to do, depending on how I fare. It'll just be on the floor, about where it was when you were holding it. Since it isn't licensed, they'll be a while connecting it to you."

His eyes found me and were tortured things. "Oh hell. Oh Jesus. Hammer… why are you helping me, after last night?"

I grinned at him. "I intend to charge you a pile of dough when you turn forty… but that only happens if I clear you. Understand, the cops won't be looking for you, not right away."

He didn't quite follow that. "Then why am I hiding out?"

"Because somebody is alternately killing and framing you Dunbars." I shrugged. "You could go into police custody, is another option."

He shook his head vigorously and was immediately sorry he had.

Out in the reception area, I used the handkerchief on the receiver when I called Velda. Within twenty minutes she was waiting in her little red Mustang at the bottom of the back stairs, admittedly not the most inconspicuous ride for spiriting away a murder suspect. But it would have to do.

I walked Dex down, gave Velda a look that said this situation was damn tight, got an I-have-this-covered nod in return, and went back up to call the State Police.

I got patched through to Corporal Jim Sheridan, who was again in the area, making it to the Hines & Carroll offices within twenty minutes, during which time my efforts to find the Dunbar living trust in the files proved fruitless.

I gave Sheridan the story as I'd outlined it to Dex Dunbar, and the trooper's words seemed to accept it but his eyes stayed skeptical.

"How long between your phone call with the victim," Sheridan asked, "and when you got here?"

"A little under two hours. Plenty of time for him to get himself killed."

"Did you call immediately after you found him?"

I shook my head. "No. That body was brand-new, the blood not even dry. I checked the whole office out first."

That should cover me if anybody saw me go in the place.

I was there a while. As a courtesy if nothing else, the Monticello cops were called to the scene, though it quickly became clear that the State Police's Bureau of Investigation would be handling the case.

Toward that end, Sergeant Virgil Bullard showed up to question me. We'd met briefly the night before last, after I found Wake, but the sergeant really wanted to get to know me today.

Bullard was stocky and round-faced and wore an ill-fitting brown suit his wife probably ordered from a Sears catalogue; the too-wide yellow-green-and-brown striped tie seemed a ghost of Christmas past. He spat a little when he talked.

"We heard all about you up here, Hammer," he said. His voice was an off-key baritone. "You have a reputation for playing fast and loose with the law."

I was in a chair in the Hines & Carroll outer office. Bullard was pacing, third-degree style. I was smoking a Lucky. Bullard was smoking a nickel cigar—giving him the benefit of the doubt, anyway.

"When you say 'law,'" I said, "do you mean cops, or statutes? Just wondering."

"We heard about your mouth, too. About how comical you can be, playing tough."

I let the Lucky ride my smirk. "I'm flattered."

"You find two corpses in three days? How do you explain that?"

"Everybody has to take a day off now and then."

It went on like that, him letting fly with dumb questions and spittle while turning various shades of red, me not giving a shit.

But Bullard insisted I be taken to the State Police station that Sheridan worked out of, and in an interview cubicle he questioned me again and again, wanting to know everything about my investigation into the Jamison Elder death, and making noises about jailing me as a material witness.

I could have called an attorney, but I didn't know any live ones in Monticello. So I just stuck to my story, which was basically true, except for skipping the part where Dex Dunbar was on the floor with a .38 in his fingers.

By the time I got back to the Dunbar place, the moon was high and I was low, really dragging. I saw no sign of Dorena downstairs and went on up to bed. In my skivvies, I crawled under the covers, and it probably took me all of twenty seconds to fall asleep.

The mattress giving and the bedsprings squeaking sent me reaching for my .45 under the pillow on the other side of the double bed.

Then I heard Dorena's voice, soft but strained in the near dark: "Mike, I'm sorry to disturb you, but… I just heard on the radio, Clarence Hines was *murdered.*

They say you found the body! This is madness! What in God's name is going on?"

I sat up in bed, reached past her to switch on the nightstand lamp, then gave it to her straight, minus only the name of the motel that I had stashed her half-brother in under Velda's care. She listened like a wide-eyed child hearing a bedtime story, only she was no child—she was a beautiful grown woman in a silk sashed robe the color of a pink pearl. No coral lipstick, no make-up at all, and the blonde hair was tousled. But she was perfection.

"Thank you," she said.

"For what?"

"Helping my brother. Dex is no killer."

"I agree."

Then she crawled up onto the bed and curled up in my arms, a petite package of warm femininity. She was crying, even sobbing, saying, "It's a nightmare… such an awful nightmare…"

I had no intention of doing anything but comfort her when suddenly her mouth was on mine, hot and hungry, salty from her tears, desperate and needing. That went on a while, then she drew away and crawled off the bed and I figured that was it.

But she clicked off the nightstand lamp, and now the only illumination was moonlight filtering through the window, making the pink-pearl robe seem to glow. She unsashed the thing, let it slip down over the stark nakedness of her, the ivory-edged slender curves, the pert breasts, the narrow waist, the dancer's legs. With the robe pooled at her feet, an arm across her breasts, leaning gently, she was *September Morn* come to life, her hand demurely concealing where her thighs met. Then she swallowed and straightened and eased the flesh fig leaf away to reveal the tufted blonde triangle. She was trembling.

So was I.

"You don't have to do this," I said.

She smiled a little and got onto the bed and crawled like a prowling cat over to me. She flipped the covers down and saw what she was after and her lovely face descended. After seconds that were an eternity of pleasure, she climbed on and straddled me, guiding me into her.

"I… I haven't done this for a while," she said shyly, or anyway as shyly as the circumstances would allow.

"Take it slow," I advised.

She did. Very slow, rhythmic, hypnotic, her head back, her eyes rolled back, her body swaying, her breathing building, and by the time she reached the finish we had surged to a crazy crescendo in a two-person bolero that no orchestra could rival.

Then she collapsed into my arms and held me, hugged me, tenderly, and just when I thought she'd gone to sleep right there on top of me, she pulled back, smiled an impish sad smile, gave me a quick kiss and ran out of there, snatching up the silk robe along the way, a jiggling vision painted in moonlight,

THE WILL TO KILL

blurring out of the bedroom.

I got up and went into the john and did some things, including splash water in my face, which looked back at me in the mirror, ashamed of itself.

Here I put Velda on the firing line, send her undercover into a mob casino, dispatch her to hole up with a guy I was *pretty sure* wasn't a murderer, and this was the thanks she got?

"You're a heel," my face told me.

I didn't argue with it.

And when I went back to bed my mind gave me a hard time, too. Guilty thoughts about Velda churned, even though she and I had a sort of understanding, but also the pieces of this thing were floating in my head, swimming there, tumbling, turning, a jigsaw puzzle that refused to assemble itself.

Maybe an hour later, I sat up in bed, frustrated and tired but with no possibility of sleep. Switched on the nightstand lamp and got into my shirt and trousers, shoes and socks, too. The only way to cure sleeplessness like this was to go out in the night air and walk it off.

The way I had not so long ago, when I came upon half a corpse floating in the Hudson.

Maybe that memory was why I stuck the .45 in my waistband.

CHAPTER ELEVEN

The moon wasn't full any more, but there was enough of it left to wash the world white, with blue highlights lending impressionistic touches to the landscape that the late Wake Dunbar might well have appreciated.

The few remaining clumps of snow here and there, the patches of brown grass trying to be green again, made for unearthly terrain for me to tread along. Earlier today, what with the spring thaw, the ground could get muddy in places; but at night, with the temperature down to fifty or maybe a little below, you could walk well enough. A little spongy, maybe, but your feet didn't sink.

Still, it was hard to believe that, just a few days before, an ice floe with half a passenger had deposited itself at my feet, as if winter had been making one last forlorn statement.

It was just chilly enough that I wondered if I should have slung on my suit coat, but mostly I didn't mind. For a man trying to walk off sleeplessness, weather this raw might not seem ideal. But I knew what I needed, and that was to trudge along, my hands in my pockets, letting the thoughts that were plaguing me tire themselves out, even as a breeze nipped at me like a dog at my heels. Just enough wind ruffled the pines surrounding the estate to whisper at me, not saying anything at all, yet taunting me still.

How the hell can you treat Velda like that?

Not the pines talking, just the tattered remnants of my conscience.

Who is behind all these murders and frame-ups? A killer on the loose, and you're just banging the cute client! Get with it, Hammer. You're not that damn old.

"Just old enough to know better," I mumbled to myself. I strolled around the edge of the woods that hugged the grounds, the big gray-stone mansion sleeping, not a light on in the place, and yet some unknown thing in the darkness seemed imminent. Something that nagged and gnawed at me, threatening to happen.

It almost seemed inevitable when sounds broke through my thoughts, distant but distinct sounds, odd sounds, *a crunch, a pause, a rattle, a crunch, a pause, a rattle.* What the hell *was* that? Familiar, but... *what?*

As I came around the far side of the house, still hugging the tree line, I could tell that the sounds emanated from the back of the carriage house. The source of the *crunch, pause, rattle* was not yet visible to me, set back as the two-story gray-stone structure was from the main building.

In the cavern of the night, however, those sounds were small but well-defined, even echoing, *crunch, pause, rattle*. I moved along the trees, and then I could see across the vast yard a figure, small, almost skeletal, digging in the middle of the night, a mobile scarecrow in the unfenced ten-by-ten garden, its brown tilled soil ready for spring to assert itself.

Who the nocturnal gardener was, I couldn't make out at this distance. Why he was at work so late at night, I couldn't say. Something was on the ground, at the edge of the waiting garden—a canvas duffel bag, the size a sailor might haul over his shoulder off and on a ship.

Obviously I needed to check this out, but if somebody was up to some malicious thing, I couldn't just come jogging across the expanse of the lawn and announce myself.

Instead, I cut back along the tree line and came around the front of the house to make my way to the carriage house, keeping close to the structure, hugging it as shadows hugged me. Edging along with my back to the outer stone wall, I did my best to stay quiet, though the sound of the shovel digging into hard ground, with shovelfuls dumped and scattered to one side, pretty well covered my approach. Then I was to the corner of the building with the garden just beyond…

…and there he was, a foot or so down in a long narrow hole he was digging, his back to me but a familiar scrawny figure in an ear-flap cap and a black-and-white-and-red plaid hunter's jacket.

Then, like a farmer out in his field, Willie Walters leaned against his shovel, taking a few moments' break, breathing hard, some raspiness in it. The thaw had made his work possible, but it was still hard going for a skinny guy in his fifties.

Soon he started digging again, a groan accompanying each crunch of the shovel blade driven by his right foot, gouging into the unforgiving earth, a heaving sigh accompanying every dumped scoop of soil. He was just getting started, but the outline of the three-foot wide, six-foot long cavity quickly became apparent.

A grave.

Who was the grave for? I wondered, but my eyes were already swinging toward that big duffel bag. A shape, possibly human, could be discerned under the canvas, knees up but recognizably a person, or something that had been a person. If Willie was behind these murders—Chester Dunbar and Jamison Elder and Wake Dunbar—was he getting so prolific that he had to start burying his corpses now?

Could that be Chickie in that canvas shroud?

If this *was* a grave, that meant Willie would have to dig the hole deep, a good six feet anyway, because in a wooded area like this, every kind of critter would go digging here for meat. So I considered biding my time. Let him get way down deep in his hole, tired as hell, wasted from the effort, before I dealt with him.

Then the duffel bag squirmed.

Jesus God—somebody was in there! Not somebody big, but somebody alive, and I could only wonder if Walters intended to kill his victim or just plant the poor soul in this garden, buried alive, human compost.

I considered shooting him right now. He deserved it. No argument on that front. And the .45 was out of my waistband and in my hand now.

But I had so many questions, and it would be a pleasure getting the answers out of him. And they might be interesting, if the screaming didn't get in the way. His motive for killing and tormenting the Dunbars might not have a damn thing to do with money—he could be a homicidal lunatic with a will to kill, who'd hidden behind his harmless caretaker facade and had his fun.

As much as I wanted to put a bullet through that ear-flap cap, I wanted answers more. Because even with Willie right in front of me, and one of his victims in a canvas bag waiting for a grave, I couldn't make the puzzle pieces fit. I needed him *alive*, goddamnit.

I stepped out from the side of the building and walked to the edge of the garden. Huffing and puffing and digging and dumping, he hadn't heard me approach. He was maybe five feet from me. When he was between crunches, I said, "Evening, Willie."

He turned in alarm, his pale blue eyes big in the wrinkled Punch-and-Judy puss, and filled with a craziness he hadn't showed me before.

I stepped closer. "What are you getting ready to plant there, Willie?"

He was just looking at me, submerged enough in the still-shallow hole to gaze up, his face a ghastly mask of fear and rage, only the mask didn't hide the real Willie Walters: this *was* the real him, a monster who'd pretended to be a man.

When he swung the shovel, I wasn't really surprised, or not enough so that I didn't duck back and protect the gun-in-hand he was going for. What I hadn't anticipated was how quick and savage he could be, leaping from the trench and swinging the shovel wildly, the blade swishing, its owner banshee-wailing. Off-balance, I fired the .45 but the slug caught the descending shovel blade, punching a hole in it that a laser beam of moonlight shot through.

He kept swinging and screaming, wildly cutting the air, and was almost on top of me, my back to the rear outer wall of the carriage house, when my next round took off the thumb of his right, clutching hand. It flew off and arced through the air and planted itself in the soil. His scream had pain in it now, and red geysered out of the thumb stump like a hose watering his twisted garden.

But the pain sent him into a frenzy, and I was just about to send one through his brain when that shovel blade finally caught me, the flat part thank God, a one-handed swing now, but the scrawny son of a bitch had enough power that my .45 got knocked to hell and gone.

That made him laugh. He laughed through the pain, his eyes crazed and bulging, his teeth bared like something feral, his shrill shrieks ripping the night, the cry of some wild creature in the woods either killing or getting killed.

I caught the handle of the shovel in both hands and yanked it out of his grasp. He stood there with a look of astonished dismay and disappointment on that crinkly, jut-jawed face, a child whose toy had been taken away by a cruel parent.

I had to step to one side to do it, but in batter-up mode, I swung the thing, and that shovel end, the backside of it, smashed him in the face. All it took was that one blow. The sound was a different crunch than his digging had made, more like stepping through a rotted board, lots of little bones and some big ones, too, cracking and snapping, and when I drew the shovel back, the face was pushed in, nose flattened, mouth open on jagged things that used to be teeth, and he wasn't jut-jawed any more. With the tip of the shovel point, I gave him a little nudge and he stumbled and tumbled backward into the shallow grave.

He'd already been dead, of course. The bones of his nose had smashed into his brain and ended his miserable excuse for a life. He should have suffered more, but you can't have everything.

Quickly I went to the squirming duffel bag. I undid the ties at its top and loosened the aperture, widening it, tugging the rough canvas gently down over a naked young woman. Hands duct-taped before her, ankles, too, her legs having been brought up in a fetal position, her mouth slashed with tape, she was dirt-splotched and bruised here and there; and cigarette burns dotted her flesh. But she had been lovely before the terror, and would be again, a dark-haired, dark-eyed doll who I cradled and rocked.

And best of all she was alive.

But I had to wonder how many like her were already buried in this garden. Missing girls soon to be tragically found.

The duct tape gag came off in one swift tug, and she looked up at me in hope that could switch to horror if I turned out to be another madman, and after all I've been accused of that.

But I kept my voice soft and soothing as I said, "You're going to be fine now. Fine."

She nodded.

"Is your name Linda Cohen?"

She swallowed and nodded, and nodded, and nodded.

"I'm going to get you back to your folks, honey," I said. "Don't you worry now."

Into my arms I lifted her as she shivered in nakedness and shock, and I carried her to the house, where Dorena was already at the back kitchen door, on the little open porch there, a number of lights on in the house now. I eased Linda onto the ground to see if she could stand; she could, but she held onto me.

In her sashed robe again but with a nightgown peeking from beneath it, Dorena rushed toward us, barefoot on the cold ground.

I said, "This is one of the missing girls. In the papers?"

She nodded. She knew at once what I was talking about, and anyway this was no time for explanations. Admirably businesslike, she slipped an arm around the Cohen girl and said, "Let's get her inside and cleaned up."

The girl swung toward me, squeezing my arm, looking up in terrible fear with the biggest brown eyes you ever saw. "There's *another* one! You have to stop the other one!"

Dorena asked, "What's she talking about?"

I said, "I think I know. I think maybe I've always known. Or anyway I should have."

Already walking the girl toward the short flight of stairs up to the kitchen door, Dorena looked back at me wide-eyed. "Mike, what are you…?"

"Give her some tender loving care, and find some clothes for her. She looks about your size."

"All right. And I'll call the police…"

I shook my head. "Not just yet. Tend to the girl here."

They were up on the little porch now, Dorena gazing at me curiously, an arm around the teeth-chattering girl's waist. "No police?"

"No. When I come back, I'll handle that."

"Back from *where*?"

"I'll be close by. Right here on the grounds. Just something that needs attending to."

I was heading off into the dark when Dorena called out again: "*Mike!*... What sick monster *did* this to her?"

"Willie Walters. He was sick, all right... so sick he died of it."

I stood at the foot of the shallow grave that Walters hadn't been able to finish before he filled it with himself. On his back, the sprawl of his arms and legs only partly in the hollowed-out rectangle, he stared up at the sky with his caved-in face frozen in dismayed surprise.

Those puzzle pieces weren't swimming now, not tumbling or turning, either—they were falling into place, clicking together, fitting nicely into a clear if bizarre image.

I stuffed a Lucky in my lips and fired it up. I let a ghostly stream of smoke seep through my teeth.

"Talk to me, Willie," I said.

And he talked to me. He didn't say a word, of course, there on his dead back with his crushed jaw and his broken teeth and his flattened nose and his blank eyes. But he spoke to me, ever so eloquently.

When I'd listened to everything he had to say, I tossed the Lucky sparking into the night, got the .45 out of my waistband again, and went around to the side door of the carriage house. The door was unlocked, as it always seemed to be, and between the comfy chairs

facing the TV a small floor lamp cast muted yellow
light onto the rec room. I wandered across the braided
rug to the bookcase for a glance at the sexy paperbacks
on display there. Those and the stack of well-thumbed
*Playboy*s on a shelf hadn't belonged to Jamison Elder,
after all. Seemed still waters *hadn't* run deep.

The .45 led me up the circular wrought-iron staircase
where the two doors awaited. I tried the one to Willie
Walters' room and found it unlocked. On first glance,
the cramped space illuminated by moonlight through
a window presented nothing of much interest—a twin
bed made with military precision, a single nightstand
with reading lamp and a few dirty paperbacks, a
mirror-less dresser with a portable radio on it, another
comfy chair.

But in the closet I found three padded sportcoats
tailored to fill out the shoulders of somebody skinny
like Willie. Only I didn't think the sportcoats were his.
Nor did I think the several pairs of elevator shoes were
Willie's, either.

On the upper closet shelf I found a box of .22 slugs
and a hip holster that a revolver of that caliber might
fit; but it was empty.

Back on the little landing, I faced the door to the
bedroom opposite and, with my left hand, tried the
door. Unlocked, if it even had a lock. I went in.

The childish bedroom took on a surreal quality, the
moonlight streaming through a window, everything
ivory tinged blue, much as the ground outside had

been. The model airplanes hanging from the ceiling in silhouette were like strange prehistoric creatures; the tee-pee in one corner lurked in darkness, though its geometric shape was discernible.

I positioned myself at the foot of the wagon-wheel bed, toward the right. The Lone Ranger bedspread was bunched at the bottom. Under only a sheet and light blanket, he was sleeping on his side, or pretending to, with his back mostly to me, his head deep in a fluffy pillow. The little angel.

"Here's a bedtime story for you, Chickie," I said.

He made the slightest movement, or perhaps that was the covers rustling from the nearby open window that cast its shaft of moonlight across the lower bed.

"Once upon a time a man had a son," I said. "He loved that son very much, but before long, when the boy was very young, the father discovered that the boy had no interest in playing with other children. But who knows? Maybe the boy was just shy. He did have hobbies, this boy—he particularly liked to torture and kill small animals, squirrels, ducks in a pond, cats, the family dog. I'm only guessing now, but he probably also liked to set fires, even burning down buildings... possibly including his inventor father's workshop... and he almost certainly lacked any remorse after, for that or any other antisocial behavior he displayed. Like lying or stealing. And he showed no warmth to his family members, this boy. In my experience, children like that often are beaten or abused by parents who don't realize that this behavior is a kind of sickness. That the lack of human feeling and emotion and understanding of responsible behavior made it as if a child like this had been born blind."

The covers rustled, but Chickie said nothing.

"But this boy, this very special boy, was luckier than most of his ilk. You see, his father had been a policeman in a big city and had seen a lot in his years on the force. He recognized the danger signs in his son. He knew that he had a budding sociopath on his hands, who might possibly even grow into a homicidal maniac one day. So he controlled the boy, kept him young, pampered and protected him, and the boy knew no other way to live and went along with what was a very unusual approach to child-rearing. Though an ex-cop, the father was now very wealthy, and could afford to hire help to look after his son, and… contain him. He lied to the world, even to some members of the family, that the boy was retarded or autistic. And he hired a good man named Jamison Elder to be the boy's handler… his companion, his teacher. The boy liked Jamison, as far as it went—the man was kind, helpful, and understood the boy's affliction. Then the boy got older and perhaps less easy to handle, so the father hired an ex-prison guard to be a kind of jailer for his son."

Movement, or wind, shifted the sheets.

"This proved to be a tragic mistake. You see, by terrible happenstance, the jailer had a similar sickness, and eventually he and the boy formed a pact, a kind of partnership. My thinking is that the boy promised the jailer money, one day… or perhaps the boy had access right now to the fifty thousand dollars a year his trust fund generated. I'll get back to how that's possible, but right now let's just celebrate a remarkable friendship— the jailer and the prisoner who became a team. Who shared a singular hobby."

Chickie said nothing.

"You see, things really changed for the boy when he hit puberty. He had new feelings surging within his somewhat childish frame. He had new interests, new… desires. It's very likely he became a voyeur, window-peeping on the two beautiful women who lived in the main house, likely making use of that old-fashioned spy glass over there. And so, with his friend the jailer, he undertook a new interest, a new hobby that beat drowning ducks all to hell. He put on a coat with the shoulders padded and wore elevator shoes that made him look older and more, well, normal. He was basically a good-looking boy, after all, and had a natural charisma when he unleashed it. He'd seen enough TV to know how to behave with people. The boy, with the help of his jailer friend, went trolling through the clubs and resorts here in the Catskills and lured lovely young women into his clutches… corny way to put it, I know, but so very apt… and brought them somewhere, possibly somewhere on the grounds here, and pursued his new hobby. Torture, rape, and worse… How could anything be worse? How about burying these girls, once they'd been used, in that garden out there? *Burying them alive.*"

Chickie said nothing, though the cover shifted slightly. The gun missing from Willie's shelf—was it in Chickie's hands, under those covers? That would be fine. That would make it self-defense.

"Things went well with the new hobby, for several years, but then the boy's other companion… the one who'd been so close to him, so good to him, the family servant, his teacher, his friend… learned something he shouldn't have. He became aware, to what extent we'll never know, of the hobby the boy and his jailer cohort pursued. And this good man panicked and fled, knowing he was in danger. He had to get away from this place, from these grounds, and he lied and said he had a sick sister he had to go see, and he got away from this horror, with only the vaguest plans about what he'd do to fix the problem. Oddly, he loved the boy, like the late father… who the boy had also killed, playing on his caring parent's heart condition to do so. This family servant considered the boy a freak of nature whose evil inclinations were no fault of his own. This he was sorting out as he drove into the night, rushing to an appointment with an ice floe."

Chickie said nothing.

"Getting back to that fifty thousand a year that the boy may have had access to, I admit I am speculating. Of course, much of this is speculation, but I'm confident doors to terrible rooms will soon be flung open by the authorities and others. One such door may well open on another of the boy's friends, a lawyer who controlled the estate, who perhaps had been dipping into the funds himself and could use a new friend, like the boy. At his discretion, the lawyer could give the boy his yearly fifty-grand stipend. But I think more was going on than just that."

The sheets, the thin blanket, rustled.

"I think a second alliance, between the lawyer and the boy—possibly not involving the jailer at all—led to attempts on the lives of his siblings. This would clear the way to an even greater fortune one day. This scheme included framing a sister-in-law for the murder of one brother, and—revealing the boy's ability to protect himself, when a snooping detective threatened to upset things—also framing the *other* brother… for the murder of the family lawyer, who might have objected to some of the boy's more outlandish machinations of late. A lot of clever little touches accompanied these efforts—the punctured brake hose, the broken studio step, gunshots in the night, even lying and saying a sibling who showed no previous interest in him had come around to watch TV with the boy, and of course tried to gas him to death. That detective I mentioned got conned by the jailer into checking on the boy, who had turned the gas on himself, shortly beforehand."

The sheet flipped a little. That was the wind. Wasn't it?

"The boy knew it would be unwise to add his nice sister to the list of deaths and murder frame-ups. But he could handle her. Maybe he liked to watch her, when she didn't know it. Anyway, he knew one day he would be able to fool the doctors, too, and he would break out of this prison of an endless childhood imposed upon him by the father he had so gladly murdered. That was probably the final tip-off for me, champ—that you did not have a photo anywhere of your beloved late father. For all your talk of heaven, you just don't feel a thing, do you? You never have."

Slowly I walked around the bed.

"But, Chickie, despite your *New York Times* crossword smarts, you really are just a dumb kid at heart. Sending me those show-off taunting letters is a good example of that. You've improvised too much these last few days, and the police will find you out. What bugs me is that you probably *will* be considered crazy or mentally deficient, and wind up in some hospital where one day you can bluff your way out. That I can't allow. Because here's where your luck ran out, Chickie my boy—*I'm a killer too.*"

I came around and thrust the gun toward the sleeping boy… but he wasn't sleeping, was he?

Yes, he was on his side and peaceful, his expression placid.

But a pillow, used in part as a makeshift silencer, lay on the floor with a scorched hole in it, from having been pressed into the sleeping man/child's face and a gun fired into it. The bullet had gone in clean in his forehead, a small round black-red puncture, but that fluffy pillow his head was buried in would conceal the larger jagged outlet in the back of his skull through which a gory jelly made from his once-clever brain had been spewed.

CHAPTER TWELVE

Corporal Jim Sheridan got to the Dunbar estate in about thirty minutes, but the Monticello cops beat him by half of that, with an ambulance from the local hospital on their heels. The morgue wagon came flying in, too, as if that mattered.

By the time Bullard of the B.C.I. got there, the moonlight circus was in full sway—uniform and plainclothes officers sweeping the grounds, the lights atop squad cars painting the night red and blue, a photographer recording the garden while Willie's remains were still on display, then doing the same with Chickie and his bedroom, flash-bulbs strobing the carriage house second-floor windows like indoor lightning.

Sheridan and I shook hands. Even in the middle of the night, the tall, rugged trooper looked crisp in his gray uniform and purple-banded Stetson.

I walked him into the Dunbar kitchen and got him a cup of coffee while he called the Cohen girl's parents to give them the mostly good news—whatever hell that poor kid had been put through was eclipsed by her surviving it. He advised them (they were still staying at Kutsher's) to go directly to the hospital in Monticello, as their daughter was about to leave by ambulance for there.

After he hung up the phone, Sheridan said to me, "You know, Pat Chambers has a hell of a friend in you. It's going to mean a lot to him, you clearing all of this up."

Dorena was sitting over at the kitchen table, looking catatonic. I'd told her, when the cops were on the way, that Chickie had been killed, possibly by Willie Walters. And she'd got the picture from Linda Cohen that Chickie and Willie had been the girl's tag-team tormenters.

Softly I said to Sheridan, "I don't know. Pat may not be so thrilled to learn his friend's own kid bumped him off."

The trooper shook his head. "The bad guys decide who they are, Mike. We don't."

Before the Cohen girl was eased by attendants into the back of the emergency vehicle, she asked to see me. I went over and gave her a rumpled grin.

"You're going to be all right, kid," I said.

She was already in a hospital gown. "I don't... don't know about that. But I *do* know I owe you... I owe you everything."

Then she threw her arms around me and held me tight. I patted her back as she sobbed into my chest. She was going to make it. Even after what those two sorry excuses for male humans had put her through, she could still hug an ugly guy like me. It wouldn't be easy, but she'd put this nightmare behind her.

I went inside to see how Dorena was doing and found her still at the kitchen table, drinking coffee, looking pretty shell-shocked.

I sat with her a while, not saying anything, but with my hand on hers, patting, squeezing, offering occasional inadequate words of support. Her eyes were red. She'd been crying for Chickie. I supposed somebody had to.

Upstairs, I once again threw water in my face and got into my sportcoat and jammed my hat on my head, making myself borderline presentable. Anyway, it had started to get cold out there. Then I went out into a world bustling with cops and lab boys and such.

The B.C.I. processed the two crime scenes, in a preliminary fashion at least. Meanwhile, both Sheridan and Bullard wanted to hear my story. As we stood in a three-man huddle near the carriage house, I gave it to them, more or less, though all I said about Chickie was that I found the body. I could tell Bullard wondered if I'd killed the boy/man, but he didn't come right out and say so. Still, that made him a better judge of character than I'd have given him credit for.

He didn't give me a free ride, though. In the same

ill-fitting Sears suit and unfortunate Christmas tie, the stocky detective studied me with the skeptical narrowed eyes of a father appraising his daughter's prom date.

"So," he said, chewing on the stub of a cigar that had long since gone out, "you caved the prick's face in with a shovel, huh? How the hell are you going to make a self-defense plea out of that?"

I showed him the bruised area on my right wrist, where Willie's shovel had knocked the .45 from my hand, and said, "He was swinging the goddamn thing at me, and I grabbed it from him and swung back. See if any jury objects to me doing that to a raping kidnapper."

Bullard saw my point, and so did Sheridan, who even smiled a little. Cops are all about dark humor.

"So you kill the prick and rescue the girl," Bullard said, "and you find the dead kid in bed. But what does that add up to?"

When I hesitated, Sheridan said, "Isn't it obvious, Sergeant? Hammer here started sniffing around the Chet Dunbar and Jamison Elder deaths—which we now know are murders—and Willie got spooked. He bumped off his accomplice, young Charles 'Chickie' Dunbar, and was getting ready to bury their latest, and last, victim when Mike interceded."

Bullard winced in thought. "What, and then Willie would have packed up and left? Just split the scene?"

The trooper shrugged. "Works for me."

Bullard squinted in my direction. "Work for you, Hammer?"

I shook my head. "All due respect to Jim here, it smells."

Sheridan pushed his Stetson back on his head. "Why so, Mike?"

"Willie was no criminal mastermind, but he was smarter than *that*. That fresh grave in the garden would get noticed right away. His sudden absence after Chickie's murder would peg him as the immediate prime suspect. And odds are it was Willie's gun that was used on Chickie. You'll find an empty holster and a box of .22 slugs in his closet."

Bullard grunted. "Maybe *you* did the kid, Hammer."

So he'd finally turned his suspicion into words.

"He was no kid, Bullard. He was a man of twenty who'll go down in the record books as a mass murderer and sex deviant. You want to bet there aren't at least another half dozen girls buried in that garden?"

Bullard rolled the cigar stub around in his mouth. "No bet," he said softly.

A young trooper came rushing up to Sheridan; his face, with its stunned expression, would have seemed pale even without the moonlight. "Corporal, there's something you should see…"

The shaken trooper led us down the gentle slope to the fieldstone guardhouse near the gate, from which Willie had kept watch. A light was on in the little cottage. Another cop was standing outside the door, not as young as the one who'd summoned us, but just as pale. He looked like he was either about to puke or just had.

Lit by a single hanging bulb, the interior was nothing fancy, a dry-walled space with a wooden floor, home to a well-padded, well-worn armchair, a little refrigerator, a space heater, and a cot. The latter had been pushed aside, when the place was searched apparently, revealing a two-foot by two-foot metal floor hatch. The lid of it was leaned back, opening onto darkness. Wooden basement-style stairs yawned down, swallowed up after a few steps.

"An old storm cellar?" Sheridan wondered.

"Storage for preserves maybe?" Bullard suggested.

"Not any more, I don't think," I said.

As we peered down into blackness, the young trooper held out a flashlight to his corporal. "You'll need this, sir."

Flash in hand, Sheridan descended and Bullard and I followed. When we were down there, we made a crowd in the modest chamber, the floor space similar to the above. Sheridan sent the beam of light around.

We were in a cement-walled cellar with a hard dirt floor. Hugging one wall was an old, beat-up mattress like something from an army barracks. Two dog dishes, one with some water, the other empty, were near the bed. A bucket was in a corner, redolent of excrement and urine.

"Lord," Bullard said.

Sheridan's flashlight revealed something even worse. Screwed into the walls were chains and steel cuffs, for wrists and ankles.

The seasoned trooper shuddered. "I've seen enough."

We all had.

Back out in the night, which felt cool and cleansing, Bullard said, "Off the record? If you *did* kill that 'kid,' Hammer, I don't give a good goddamn."

"I still say the caretaker killed his accomplice," Sheridan said. "If Mike's right that Willie's gun is the murder weapon, we may find it on the grounds somewhere—the woods maybe, where it got flung. We'll search tomorrow."

By four a.m., the carriage house had been sealed and the garden roped off. In the daylight, the grim digging would begin. No back hoe for that garden of death, whose crop would be evidence, some of it almost certainly corpses—this job would take men with shovels, muscle, and a lot of care. Also, strong stomachs.

Vehicles began leaving, in no hurry but glad to go. The firm-jawed trooper was the last. He was about to get in his patrol car when he paused to say, "Look for us around seven."

I managed a grin. "With luck, maybe some of you guys can get three hours sleep."

"You hold down the fort till then, Mike. As a licensed private investigator in the state of New York, you're an officer of the court."

"Remind your B.C.I. pal of that," I said.

Then I was alone, and if you didn't notice the seal on the carriage house door or the rope on pegs all around the garden, everything seemed the same as it had before I'd gone out for my late-night walk.

Dorena was asleep at the kitchen table now, her head on her arms like a kid resting at a school desk.

I leaned in, gave her a gentle nudge and whispered in her ear, "They're gone. You better get some real sleep—they'll be back before you know it."

She nodded as she sat up. Got unsteadily to her feet. Stretched and yawned. She was still in the robe and, despite it all, looked lovely. We made our way to the front stairs, which were wide enough for me to walk beside her if I stayed close.

"Do you need company," I asked, "or are you all right?"

"I'm all right."

It didn't sound very convincing, but I didn't argue with her.

I walked her to her bedroom door and she gave me a hug, much like the one Linda Cohen had bestowed upon me. Then she slipped into her room with a tiny smile and tinier wave.

In the bedroom that had been Chester Dunbar's, I set the .45 on the nightstand and got out of my sportcoat. Slipped off my shoes. Then I pulled up a chair and sat backwards on it, by the window, looking out.

I should have been dead tired. Hell, I *was* dead tired. But my mind, my goddamn mind, wouldn't let me alone. The puzzle pieces had all come together, hadn't they? What was there to think about? Weren't the two monsters dead?

I considered calling Velda, but at this time of night—of morning—I chose not to disturb her sleep. In a few hours, I'd relieve her of her babysitting chores and she would return to the city, while I'd send Dex back out into the cold cruel world where maybe he'd be a drunk again and somebody else would take his gambling money, but he wouldn't be a murder suspect. Not after I coached him a little and we got our stories straight.

Not with Chickie Dunbar and Willie Walters on hand to share the gory glory.

As for me, I'd have to stick around Monticello for a day or two to help the cops, and to get Madeline Dunbar properly sprung. And there would be occasional treks back up here to deal with the legal aftermath. But I would never have to sleep in the murdered father's bedroom again. I had secured my release from the maelstrom of murder, betrayal, deceit, and madness that swirled about the Dunbar estate.

Rising, sighing, I figured I'd give the bed a try. That was when I glimpsed the ghostly figure out the window, moving quickly across the vast backyard, apparently headed for the trees.

I shoved the .45 in my waistband and moved quick, stepping into my shoes. The puzzle pieces shifted and flipped and the picture became as clear, finally, as it was disturbing. I didn't bother to check Dorena's room because I knew she wasn't there.

She was the ghostly figure, a blonde vision in a pink-pearl gown glowing white in the night.

When I hit the cool outside air, however, I didn't run. I didn't have to. She was gliding up ahead of me across the moon-swept landscape, the robe flowing like a bridal train. On the still-hard ground, in my gum soles, I didn't make much of any sound at all. She didn't even hear me till she had reached the edge of the woods and I was right behind her.

She froze for a moment, then swung around, a hand tucked behind her, her eyes wide with alarm, her mouth making a silent, "*Oh!*"

"I like to walk at night, too," I said.

"Mike! You scared me."

"Sorry. Just wondered what you were doing out here. Haven't we both had enough excitement for one night?"

Her smile was as nervous as it was unconvincing. "I suppose we have. But it's hard to sleep, after…"

"After killing Chickie?"

Her eyes got wider yet, and the way she drew her breath in, I might have punched her in the belly.

One hand was still behind her back; the other came up as a fist that she bit, then lowered. "How can you *think* that, Mike? I *loved* that boy. After Daddy died, I was the only one in that house who felt a single thing for him. His death… it's awful… it's a terrible, terrible tragedy…"

I smiled at that. "No one really talked to you tonight, did they? Not the state cops, not the local ones. But you get the picture. You know that the naked, abused girl I dropped in your lap had been tortured by your little brother and was slated by him and his buddy Walters for a garden burial. I mean, you've known all along that brother Charles was a sociopath."

She shook her head a little. "I... I don't even know what that is."

"Your father trusted you. He knew those two flawed half-siblings of yours wouldn't understand Chickie's... condition. But *you* would, he thought."

Her chin was crinkling, tears on the way. "Why would I... why would *I* kill Chickie? Even if you're right about what you say he was... socio-something— what *is* that, like a psycho?"

"A rose by any other name." I let out a hollow laugh. "You see, somebody like me—a detective—has to look at every possibility. Has to think everything through. Try to make the puzzle pieces fit. And I thought I'd done that. That I could see the picture clearly. But sometimes puzzle pieces can come together in more than one way."

Something indignant came into her expression, though fear remained at its edges. "I... I don't know what you're *talking* about. It's cold out here. I want to go back in the house."

She took a step and I blocked her.

"I wonder," I said, "if you were aware of the sick games Willie and Chickie were playing with the girls they grabbed. I like to think you weren't. But maybe you got wise to what Chickie and lawyer Hines were up to—working to remove Wake, Madeline, and Dex from their respective shares of the family fortune. And certainly you must have guessed that Chickie was responsible for Jamison Elder's demise. But what about your father?"

Her chin came up. "I *loved* my father!"

I nodded. "I think you did. Hell, I *know* you did. That may be what made it possible for you to finally remove his murderer from the face of the earth. Of course, there's another possibility."

She was shaking her head again, more vigorously now. "None of this is right. You're not getting *any* of it right…"

"What if *you* were planning to kill or otherwise remove your half-brothers from the inheritance sweepstakes? Murdering Wake, pinning it on Madeline, taking them both out of the money. And what if Hines got wise or greedy and you had to get rid of him as well, but did so very cleverly, by eliminating the lawyer and Dex at once, with your half-sib framed for a capital crime? Even if Dex didn't get the chair, he would become ineligible for his inheritance, having killed the executor of his father's estate in a scheme to expand his trust fund. And who better to blame for all of this mayhem, should it be found out, than your brother Chickie? Your own handy-dandy in-house psycho, perfect to take the blame."

Her hand swung around from behind her back and the gun in it—a .22 revolver—thrust itself at me.

"Ah," I said. "Willie's gun."

Her hand with the gun in it was shaking. "Yes, Willie's gun. But none of the rest of what you're saying is true!" Tears left her eyes to find her cheeks. "*None* of it! Yes, yes, yes… I killed Chickie. But I did it with love. Can someone like you believe that, Mike? Can you comprehend such a thing? I loved that boy despite it all!"

I frowned. "Even though you knew about the abducted girls?"

"*No!* No. God, no. I *didn't* know! I knew my brother was bad, some would even call him *evil*, but… capable of something like that? Oh my God, no. If… if only I'd killed him sooner. I thought about it often, but I waited too long. You see, Mike, it wasn't murder, not really. Not murder at all. It was… a mercy killing."

She was sobbing now. Shaking. When I batted the gun from her hand, it was like swatting a mosquito.

Dorena jumped a little, then fell to her knees and covered her face with her hands. Tears seeped through her fingers.

"What… what now, Mike? I did it. I did it, I did it, I did it. I *admit* I did it. *I killed my brother Chickie!* What next? Hand me over to the police? Or do *you* kill *me*, now?"

I took a step away from her, picked up the .22 and wiped it clean on my shirt, and tossed the gun into the trees, where on its way it broke branches and ruffled leaves before landing with a distant thud for the cops to find.

Then I went over and put an arm around her and

began walking her to the house.

"No, honey," I said. "I just wanted to thank you for saving me the trouble."

A TIP OF THE PORKPIE

Because my approach to completing Mickey Spillane's unfinished novels is to set them in the period during which he began them, I find myself working from materials that were contemporary to my famous co-author but which require me to forge a novel that is a period piece bordering on an historical novel.

I won't attempt to credit the many Internet websites that provided background on the Catskills area that provides the setting for this novel. But I am nonetheless grateful.

Some readers may realize a sort of inside joke was afoot regarding the inventions credited to Chester Dunbar and Condon Hale. The actual inventors were the unlikely show business figures of movie star Hedy Lamarr, Groucho's brother Zeppo Marx, and ventriloquist Paul Winchell.

Thank you to attorney Steve Kundel, my friend and bandmate, although any legal irregularities in this novel are mine alone.

I also wish to thank and acknowledge my wife Barb Collins, with whom I write a very un-Spillane-like mystery series about antiquing, who gave me valuable editorial suggestions all along the way. Thanks also to my partner Jane Spillane, Titan editor Miranda Jewess, my lost brother Nick Landau, and my friend and agent, Dominick Abel.

ABOUT THE AUTHORS

MICKEY SPILLANE and **MAX ALLAN COLLINS** collaborated on numerous projects, including twelve anthologies, three films, and the *Mike Danger* comic book series.

SPILLANE was the bestselling American mystery writer of the 20th century. He introduced Mike Hammer in *I, the Jury* (1947), which sold in the millions, as did the six tough mysteries that soon followed. The controversial P.I. has been the subject of a radio show, comic strip, and several television series, starring Darren McGavin in the 1950s and Stacy Keach in the '80s and '90s. Numerous gritty movies have been made from Spillane novels, notably director Robert Aldrich's seminal film noir, *Kiss Me Deadly* (1955), and *The Girl Hunters* (1963), in which the writer played his own famous hero.

COLLINS has earned an unprecedented twenty-two Private Eye Writers of America "Shamus" nominations, winning for the novels *True Detective* (1983) and *Stolen Away* (1993) in his Nathan Heller series, and for "So Long, Chief," a Mike Hammer short story begun by Spillane and completed by Collins. His graphic novel *Road to Perdition* is the basis of the Academy Award-winning Tom Hanks/Sam Mendes film. As a filmmaker in the Midwest, he has had half a dozen feature screenplays produced, including *The Last Lullaby* (2008), based on his innovative Quarry novels, also the basis of *Quarry*, a current Cinemax TV series. As "Barbara Allan," he and his wife Barbara write the "Trash 'n' Treasures" mystery series (recently *Antiques Fate*).

Both Spillane (who died in 2006) and Collins have received the Private Eye Writers life achievement award, the Eye, and the Mystery Writers of America "Grandmaster" Edgar.

MIKE HAMMER NOVELS

In response to reader request, I have assembled this chronology to indicate where the Hammer novels I've completed from Mickey Spillane's unfinished manuscripts fit into the canon. An asterisk indicates the collaborative works (thus far). J. Kingston Pierce of the fine website The Rap Sheet pointed out an inconsistency in this list (as it appeared with *Murder Never Knocks*) that I've corrected.

M.A.C.

I, the Jury
*Lady, Go Die!**
The Twisted Thing (published 1966, written 1949)
My Gun Is Quick
Vengeance Is Mine!
One Lonely Night

MIKE HAMMER

The Big Kill
Kiss Me, Deadly
Kill Me, Darling*
The Girl Hunters
The Snake
Complex 90*
The Big Bang*
The Will to Kill*
Murder Never Knocks*
The Body Lovers
Survival... Zero!
Kiss Her Goodbye*
The Killing Man
Black Alley
King of the Weeds*
The Goliath Bone*

KILL ME, DARLING
MICKEY SPILLANE & MAX ALLAN COLLINS

Mike Hammer's secretary and partner Velda has walked out on him, and Mike is just surfacing from a four-month bender. But then an old cop turns up murdered, an old cop who once worked with Velda on the NYPD Vice Squad. What's more, Mike's pal Captain Pat Chambers has discovered that Velda is in Florida, the moll of gangster and drug runner Nolly Quinn.

Hammer hits the road and drives to Miami, where he enlists the help of a horse-faced newspaperman and a local police detective. But can they find Velda in time? And what is the connection between the murdered vice cop in Manhattan, and Mike's ex turning gun moll in Florida?

"[O]ne of his best, liberally dosed with the razor-edged prose and violence that marked the originals." *Publishers Weekly*

"For Mike Hammer's fans—yes, there are still plenty of them out there—it's a sure bet." *Booklist*

"It's vintage peak-era Spillane so seamless it's hard to see where the Spillane ends and the Collins picks up." *Crime Time*

For more fantastic fiction, author events,
competitions, limited editions and more

VISIT OUR WEBSITE
titanbooks.com

LIKE US ON FACEBOOK
facebook.com/titanbooks

FOLLOW US ON TWITTER
@TitanBooks

EMAIL US
readerfeedback@titanemail.com